CHECKING IT TWICE

A SAPPHIC CHRISTMAS ROMANCE

LUCY BEXLEY

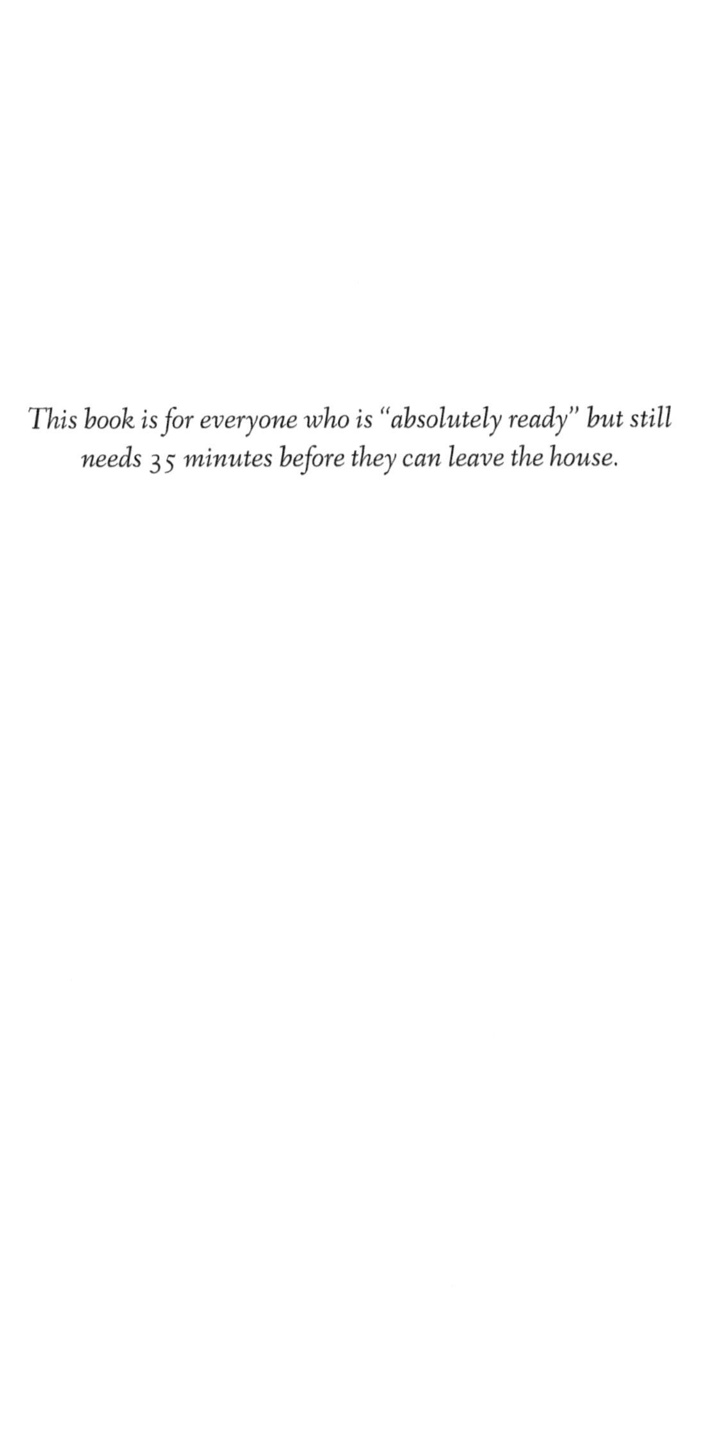

This book is for everyone who is "absolutely ready" but still needs 35 minutes before they can leave the house.

CONTENTS

SYNOPSIS

Sacha Brighton is dreading her sister's Christmas Eve wedding, but she's headed to their family cabin in Northern Michigan all the same. Though she is running several hours late and her phone battery died somewhere on the interstate. Nothing surprising there. Sacha had braced herself for a lot of diva wedding antics from Alexis. What she wasn't prepared for was to find her sister hired an androgynous wedding planner that Sacha can't get off her mind.

Hal (Hallie) Halliday (she knows) lives by her checklists. All she wants is for this wedding she's been organizing for months to go perfectly. She went to school with the Brighton sisters but has had a major glow up since her ponytail jock days and she finally feels at home in her own skin. She knew Sacha would be at the wedding. But she was still shocked to find her massive crush from high school resurrected the second she saw her. Could Hal really have a chance with Sacha?

Or will Sacha be just one more disaster Hal will have to take care of to keep this wedding on track?

Checking It Twice is a low-angst sapphic Christmas romance filled with ice skating, failed gingerbread cookies, and people trying their best.

CHAPTER 1
SACHA

Sacha had forgotten the three most important items on her packing list: her valium, her vibrator, and the verse she was supposed to recite at her sister's wedding. And she frankly couldn't see a way she'd get through this week without any of them. But they were all back in Detroit, in her apartment full of unpacked boxes. She knew exactly where they were—sitting on her nightstand where she couldn't miss them with bright orange "don't forget me" post-it notes on them. Either way, they were no use to her now as she drove through the deserted back roads up north.

Everything outside of her car looked the same, which meant she was getting close to the cabin. Bits of ice blue lake pierced the pine and birch trees. An aggressively cheery sun bounced off the inch of fresh snow blanketing the ground. She shivered and turned up the heater.

It was absurd that her family called this vacation house a cabin, a flail at humility. The *cabin* had eleven bedrooms and a four-car garage all meticulously crafted to look rustic. It was like the lake at the bottom of the hill was a funhouse mirror stretching all the modest log cabins that surrounded into extravagant mansions. But then again, everything here was a distortion of real life.

Sacha still wasn't sure why she left Chicago after her breakup with Jen a few months ago, but if she was going to stay in Michigan, she really needed to get a car of her own. It still felt weird to be driving after so many years taking the train. At least the roads this far north were mostly deserted except for the occasional deer or pickup truck.

Dolly's voice on the radio was balancing the bumpy dirt roads pitted with ice currently rattling her thoughts. Her economy rental was managing the turbulence well enough. Why did the website show so many car options when they always stick you with a red Ford Fiesta in the end? As the car wove along the snowy roads lined with evergreen forest, she imagined it looked like a Christmas ornament on a giant tree.

Christmas was meant to be spent alone. Walking the empty streets of a city she'd never been to before. Anywhere but where she was currently headed.

Sacha turned up the radio another click and sang along with the chorus. She always let Dolly do the real heavy lifting. It was the sort of cathartic emotional fuck you she needed to get her through her sister's holiday wedding. And another family Christmas. Single. Again.

She'd been driving for nearly three hours. This drive had given her too much time to cycle through all of the reasons she shouldn't have come back to Michigan in the first place. And she definitely shouldn't be spending Christmas with her family even if her sister was getting married on Christmas Eve. It was just like Alexis to try to rebrand a holiday as her own.

If she didn't get there by the time Jolene ended, Sacha promised herself she would turn this car around and drive all the way back to her lonely apartment in Corktown like a father making good on his family vacation threat.

She slowed and flicked on her blinker, laughing to herself because there was no one around to signal her intentions to but the deer in the woods and the hawks circling overhead.

The tires bounced like landing gear as they made contact with the first paved surface in what felt like 100 miles. The driveway made a lazy, winding path up the hill. There wasn't a speck of snow or ice on the black surface, just its snakelike body slithering toward the house. Only time would tell if it was poisonous. She laughed at her own dramatic thought. Not the best sign if she was already reverting to her sullen teenage self before she'd even stepped foot on the property.

She pulled the little red Fiesta rental between a black Range Rover and an old burgundy Jeep with wood side paneling—now that was a vehicle she could see herself in. Parking reminded her of pedaling her Little Tykes car into the garage and crashing it into the space between her parents' Lexus. What was it about coming home that always sent her back to that inept place of childhood? Emotions running high, in constant need of fruit snacks and a nap.

Sacha stepped out of the car and looked at the house—three stories of glittering windows towered before her. Its Lincoln Log structure was strung with white lights that hung like icicles over the deck that wrapped around the first floor. On the lawn someone was crouched over, dealing with yet another tangle of lights. Their navy-blue sweater picked up rogue snowflakes like stars gathering in the night sky. It must be Todd, her sister's fiancé, because no one in her family would be outside doing manual labor.

She'd met Todd once at what her mother had assured

her would be "a relaxed family barbecue," but was actually a rented-out country club with a dress code her cutoff shorts had failed to adhere to. There were all these grotesque versions of what a country club might imagine a barbecue was. Gourmet hotdogs, Foie gras "sliders," croquet.

Todd had launched into a lengthy explanation of the rules of cornhole, a game Sacha had brought to the event herself, as though she hadn't spent her college weekends tailgating. As though she didn't defy her parents' wishes and go to one of the state's party schools.

When she felt sad about her sister's marriage, she sometimes remembered the delight she'd felt when she absolutely destroyed Todd at that game. His mood slid like a beanbag down the board from encouraging words on her first few shots to disbelief and impatience the second time she beat him. He hadn't spoken a word to her or anyone else for the next hour.

Probably time to mend that fence. She could go over and give him a hard time about this electric light show, clear the air before she had to spend the better part of a week around him. Simple.

He was crouched down behind a bride and groom light-up snowman set—who in their right mind would dream up something this grotesque?

His hair looked darker than she remembered. Had Alexis had him dye it for the wedding? Strange but not out of character for her sister. And his outfit looked color-coordinated in a way she didn't expect, walking a line between rugged and refined in a navy sweater and dark denim. But who else would her sister put up to such a task? And who would go along with it?

Sacha's open jacket flapped in the wind coming off the water at the far edge of the property. Her bag was light on her shoulder as she made her way across the lawn ready to make nice.

"Do you need some help, Todd?"

The figure that popped up from behind the honest-to-g gilded Santa's sleigh that the bride and groom snow people were being arranged in was decidedly not Todd. Nope. Not even the slightest bit Todd. The person stood to their full height, a few inches taller than Sacha and squinted into the sun bouncing off the snow, like sugar on a cookie.

"Sorry to disappoint you." The voice was honey warm and kind. "Did you need Todd for something?"

"Only to try to make amends before he marries my sister." She swept her hair back from her face in a way she hoped was rakish and sexy but probably more closely resembled rollercoaster damage control.

"I'm Sacha."

"I know."

"Oh... how?" And more importantly why was this dapper human putting up decorations on her parents' lawn? Their boots were an oiled dark brown leather, straddling the line between rugged and dressy. They definitely looked slightly rugged in their navy fisherman's sweater and oatmeal colored beanie. Were they some sort of sexy groundskeeper who lived in town, hired to create the illusion of a family invested in holiday cheer? And if so, who should she thank for that? Her sister?

"Well, for starters Alexis hired me to plan her wedding. And for the main course, we went to high school together. Though I was a little more feminine-leaning back then. Hal Halliday." Hal's chin lifted, showcasing a strong jaw.

An impossibly warm hand gripped Sacha's. How was this person not wearing gloves? And more importantly how had Sacha survived high school without noticing them? Did she know any Hals? She tried to run back through her high school years, but they were a haze of clove cigarettes she had pretended to like and sickly-sweet vanilla body spray she had actually loved. The olfactory memory sent a little shudder through her.

"I'm hoping that shudder isn't related to you remembering me. It's okay if you don't, by the way. Like I said I've changed a lot."

"Sorry, you must think I'm the worst. And that's really only partly true. I'm trying to place you by picturing you as more feminine, but I can't."

"Good, I wish you wouldn't. Let's just start fresh."

"Ok, fresh it is." Sacha kicked the toe of her boot into the snow, sending up a soft glittering spray. "I hope this isn't awkward, but what pronouns do you prefer?"

Hal let out an audible breath and smiled. "Trust me, as uncomfortable as that question might have felt to you, it's 100 times less awkward than your dad guessing and finally referring to me solely as champ. I use she/her, mostly." Hal pulled the beanie off of her head and mussed her wavy dark brown hair. It was short on the sides and longer on top and as Hal adjusted it Sacha couldn't stop imagining what it would look like absolutely wrecked first thing in the morning.

"Got it. Same for me." Sacha pointed to herself awkwardly. "She/her, I mean. And I'll talk to my dad about the champ business. Mild disagreements are kind of our thing."

"Nah, that's ok. I lost my dad a few years ago and I find your dad's attempts, even though he's a bit problematic, oddly comforting. Besides, he's not really arou—"

The door to the cabin flew open and the chaotic swirl of Alexis energy cut through their peace.

"Cha-cha, you made it! What took you so long? And why didn't you answer any of my calls?"

"Oh, you know, I was driving to your destination wedding in the middle of absolutely nowhere when my phone died. And please, don't call me that." Sacha pulled her phone from her coat pocket and waved its darkened screen at Alexis to punctuate her point.

"Wow, did you also throw it from your moving vehicle? How do you read anything on that shattered screen? Just, like, get a new phone."

"My screen is fine. Are you impressed that I made it to this isolated fortress relying solely on my memory and survival skills or not?"

"Fine, Tchotchke. I'm very happy to see you, I've been excited all morning. And it's not nowhere. It's the cabin. And it's only a few hours from the airport."

"Somehow that one's worse," Sacha sighed.

Alexis tiptoed her way across the snow in decidedly inappropriate suede boots. This place had two main seasons: snow and mud, and neither of them were very forgiving of suede. But Alexis was going to look good or ruin $500 dollar shoes trying. Sacha wiggled her toes in her own winter boots, white-capped with the salt of the city streets.

"How was the airport?"

"I wouldn't know. I just drove in from Detroit. I'm actually living there for a while."

Alexis narrowed her eyes. "Since when? I thought you were coming so late because you had to coordinate a flight."

"One day isn't so late. And since... a little while ago. I'm still unpacking." Technically true. Unpacking was typically a six-month project.

"So explain to me again why you're getting here so late."

"I hit a little traffic on I-75."

Alexis crossed her arms and the silence cracked between them until Sacha broke.

"And I overslept," Sacha said.

"Yes, that makes more sense. Well, you can expect me to be your personal alarm clock for the rest of this week. I have a lot for you to do, starting with calling mom and talking her down about the seating chart."

"I'm not here to work, Alexis. And you know I can't talk mom down from anything, only up and over the edge."

Alexis rolled her eyes and behind them Hal laughed quietly. Sacha glanced at her and she busied herself opening a new box of lights.

"We'll see." Alexis turned her attention toward the decorations.

"Hal, darling, do you have any lip gloss?"

"I do." Hal straightened and rummaged in a tan leather pouch at her feet, somewhere between a tool belt and a messenger bag, and pulled out a tube of cherry red gloss that she passed to Alexis. It didn't seem like Hal's shade. Hal struck Sacha as a natural lip balm type of person, clear and minty.

Alexis held out the gloss to Sacha, but she shook her head.

Hal looked up at Sacha, her eyes a mossy green, or were they more teal? "Did you need a phone charger too?" Hal asked. "I have one you can use."

"Oh, sure. Thanks."

Hal retrieved the charger in a split second like she was unholstering a weapon.

"You and that bag are my fairy godmother," Alexis said, popping her lips. The gloss shone in the sun.

"That's what I'm here for." Hal took the lip gloss back from Alexis and returned it to her bag with careful precision before zipping it shut and returning to her Griswold front yard antics.

"What do you think of this little house?" Alexis pointed to a structure about the size of a treehouse, its wooden sides made to look like gingerbread and its windows the translucent red and green of hard candies. Sacha squinted at the house, it seemed cute and unnecessary and very Alexis. "You like it, right? Hal built it for me. I wanted it to be sweet, like the adorable cottage in Hansel and Gretel."

"Do you mean where the witch lives? The place where she traps children before cooking them?"

"No, I don't think so. It's that one from the story that the kids eat pieces of."

"It's concerning to me that you don't know how completely fucked up that story is."

"It's just a cute house in the woods, Sach. Relax. Not everything is a political cause."

"You know me, out here in the land of the rich protesting fairy tales."

Alexis shook her head and threw her arm around Sacha. "You really need to stop frowning. What's wrong?"

"Nothing's wrong."

"I know you're not really upset about a fairy tale. Is it boy trouble?"

Sacha shrugged out from under Alexis's arm. "Not recently."

"Girl trouble?"

Behind them, Hal let out a cough but when Sacha glanced back, she was calmly winding lights around the sleigh.

"Not every problem is about who I'm sleeping with, you know."

"Sure. But this one is, right?"

"Ugh, yeah. Jen and I broke up a while ago."

"Well, you must be relieved."

"What? I mean I am, but why would you say that?"

"She didn't have much of a personality and you didn't seem that happy. I assumed she was just really good in bed."

"You think I stayed in a relationship for two years for Jennifer's body?"

Behind them, Hal let out another cough that was doing a horrible job of disguising her laughter. Sacha tried to hide the answering smile on her own face by frowning.

"Chin up, Sach. Maybe you'll meet someone at the wedding."

CHAPTER 2

HAL

Hal watched Sacha and Alexis head inside before returning her attention to the lights. The strings had left indents across her palms where she'd gripped them too tightly while eavesdropping and pretending to work. *Smooth*. She felt like she was back in high school, just outside the action, and yearning for the popular girl who would never notice her.

She knew Sacha would be here. Of course she did. She'd planned the guest list. Hell, she'd planned the entire week. But she'd failed to anticipate the all-encompassing reality of Sacha Brighton. The no-oxygen-in-the-great-outdoors quality of her presence. But now Sacha was here, in the exact same place as Hal and looking like *that*. She hadn't prepared herself for the Great Lake blue of her eyes that seemed like a dare. Or that she'd still glow with that slightly chaotic energy.

Hal pulled her beanie from her head and ran her hand through her short hair, a good reminder of just how far away high school was.

As she strung lights, Sacha's words about her ex pinged through Hal's body, setting off little fireworks of possibility in her stomach. *Jen.* A far cry from the jocks that used to follow Sacha around. Well, that's if she didn't include herself, but Hal's admiration had always been discrete. In a place like Michigan back then, it had to be.

Nope, not going there. She had a job to do. A job she cared about. She could get through a week of being near Sacha Brighton, especially if that week was giving her the respectable reason she needed to avoid spending the holiday with her mother.

Hal pulled her notebook from her back pocket and flipped it open to her afternoon list. She checked off "#7: *Front Lawn Decorations*" before slipping it back into her pocket. She aligned her tools neatly back in her bag alongside the lip gloss and one hundred other items Alexis might need before slinging the whole thing over her shoulder so it rested across her chest.

A quick glance at her watch as she headed inside for a shower before the first night's dinner only confirmed that she needed to be quick. Running into Sacha and then shamelessly listening into her conversation with Alexis had shifted her schedule by eight minutes. She needed time to check in with the caterer about food allergies and make sure the table was set properly. This left her with absolutely no time to think about Sacha and the way her smile was still just the slightest bit lopsided, like she was perpetually on the verge of telling a joke. Perfect. Forty-five minutes in and she was screwed and not in the good way.

Hal stepped out of the shower in the guest suite, leaning her back against the cool door as she gathered her thoughts. She had exactly eleven minutes to get dressed and be in the kitchen. Thank god for short hair. She slipped into a light binder and her favorite blue dress shirt. Her phone rang from where she had it charging on the nightstand just as she was pulling on her black dress pants. Rule number one: charge your phone at every opportunity.

Her mother's number flashed across the screen and she thought about ignoring it. She was technically working and didn't have time for the detour of a guilt trip. But ignoring only made it worse. She trailed her finger across the screen to accept the call.

"Hello?"

"Hallie, it's mom."

"Yes, I know."

On the other end of the line, her mother cleared her throat. She knew she should soften her tone, but every time she did, she regretted it immediately. "I wanted to check in again about Christmas. Your sister's getting here at 11 am. What time should we expect you? And will you be bringing a... friend this year?"

"No, I would guess all my *pals* have their own plans. But I told you last week, I can't make it this year. I'm working at Alexis Brighton's wedding."

"I heard from your sister that the wedding is on Christmas Eve, not Christmas Day."

Hal flipped open her notebook and added, "strangle Emily," to the bottom of her personal to-do list. "Yes, um, the wedding is Christmas Eve, but there's a Christmas day brunch and some other things I'll need to finish up. The work of a wedding planner isn't really done until the blissed-out couple boards that plane for the honeymoon."

"Ah, brunch, so you'll be free by what, noon? One? Just come after that."

HAL MADE it to the kitchen with 45 seconds to spare and quickly checked "confirm menu" and "perfect table setting" off of her list. She spent the next hour running around making sure everything was flawless for the first-night family dinner, checking items off her list until the only thing left was to eat.

When she popped her head out of the swinging door that separated the kitchen from the dining room, most of the Brighton family was seated. Hal scanned the table. Something felt off but she couldn't see anything immediately amiss. Sacha caught her eye and smiled. Half a second later Alexis followed Sacha's gaze and a mischievous smile spread over her face as she waved Hal over.

"This all looks amazing, Hal." Alexis glanced around the table. "You're always focused on your list, but you forgot to set a seat for yourself."

"Oh, I was just planning to eat a little something in the kitchen. I still have a few things I need to take care of tonight."

"Don't be ridiculous. You have to eat with us, especially now that Sach is here. You two should catch up."

Catch up on what, exactly? Sacha took an audible drink from her water glass, making eye contact with the chandelier.

"Ok, thanks, but only for a bit. I need to make sure everything's set for more people to arrive tomorrow afternoon, so I want to check on the guest rooms and towels."

"I promise the towels aren't going anywhere. And most

people decided to stay in town." Alexis turned to her sister. "Sacha, please move over so there's room for Hal."

"Anything you want, madame bride." Sacha scooted over without standing up like a hostage hopping the chair they're tied to across the room.

Hal pulled over a high-backed antique-looking chair with a wicker seat from the corner of the dining room. It creaked a bit as she lowered herself down, but the center held. She sat next to Sacha, trying to leave a bit of distance between them, not sure how to interpret the chair hop or really anything that was Sacha Brighton. It was no use. She could smell the sweet floral scent of her shampoo and was acutely aware of her breathing. Hal took a deep breath and reached for her drink but found nothing there. Of course, she'd need more than just a chair to eat. There wasn't even an empty place setting just lurking around because she'd made sure everything was exact.

"I'll be right back; I'm just going to grab another setting." Hal paused for a moment scanning the table. "And some more wine."

"I've got it." Sacha stood up quickly and beelined for the kitchen like she was fleeing for her safety. But she returned a few moments later with a plate and cutlery balanced on her open palm, a wine glass dangling between her fingers by the stem.

Hal watched as Sacha gingerly laid out the items on the deep green tablecloth in front of her. Her hand was warm when she touched the space between Hal's shoulder blades gently and leaned over her to fill her wine glass. Sacha's voice was low when she whispered, "You're off the clock, let someone else do something around here."

Sacha settled back into her seat and shifted to look at her sister, bringing her closer to Hal in a way that made her breath catch. The sisters exchanged looks that Hal couldn't decipher, but whatever wordless exchange they were having ended with Sacha shaking her head slightly and turning back to her wine.

Alexis cleared her throat. "So, Hal, remind me, are you seeing anyone?"

CHAPTER 3
SACHA

The dress was an abomination. The fact that it didn't fit was not a problem so much as it was a possible solution. A golden ticket out of this Christmas tree disaster of a gown.

They were in Sacha's childhood bedroom. Well, technically it was her childhood *vacation* bedroom. Even thinking that made Sacha feel ill. What kind of person had a childhood vacation bedroom? A Brighton. That's who.

The walls had been stripped bare of her pop punk posters and angsty poetry. All of it likely burned in the fireplace the second she'd gone off to college, if she knew her mother like she thought she did.

The walls were now painted a soothing, sophisticated, and all-around terrible blush color, probably called something like Yesterday's Rosé. The mirror she studied herself in was freestanding and gilded. When she'd walked in last night a monogrammed guest towel, now thrown on the floor, had been resting on top of an honest to god wash basin. It was all rather Marie Antoinette. Though that was the

Brighton way—everything looking perfect whether it had any right to or not.

Sacha studied the midnight blue nail polish on her feet, wondering if she should tell her sister not to marry Todd or just hint heavily at it.

In some ways Todd was the perfect match for Alexis. Moneyed, hair that didn't move in the wind from his speedboat. But thinking of her sister trapped in this world turned her stomach. It was right up there with last night's wine, mixing together in a swirl of possible regrets. Sure, Alexis drove her crazy, but no one deserved a lifetime of small talk over canapés.

Alexis clicked her tongue as she examined Sacha in the mirror. "You still with me Sacha? Why didn't you tell me you'd lost weight?"

"Lost weight from what? The image of me you have in your head?" The dress slipped down, revealing Sacha's lilac lace bra and she hiked it up again as she reached for her coffee.

"When I asked you for your size, you said 8. And please put that coffee down before you spill it."

"I think this dress would absorb a little spill without issue. And I thought you were asking about shoes, not whatever this is." Sacha waved her hand up and down her body like it was a blackboard she was trying to erase, but the green velvet dress with red and white trim remained. "Besides, this coffee is the only thing keeping me sane right now. This dress is evil, Alexis. I feel like an extra in The Muppet Christmas Carol. And not even one of the cool rats. You're beautiful enough without a stunt like this."

"Well, at least you think I'm beautiful." Alexis shot Sacha a saccharine smile. "I thought you liked that movie."

"Yes, when I was seven."

Alexis crossed her arms over her chest.

"Fine, I still like it," Sacha muttered.

"I know. And you'll always be seven to me, babe. I think the dress is cute *and* festive. Maybe we need another opinion. I could call Todd. Or..." Alexis raised her eyes to the ceiling like she was scrolling through a mental contacts list. "Maybe we can see what Hal thinks?"

"What? Why would we see what Hal thinks? Surely, she has things to do like match nail polish to your lingerie or something."

"Because she's my wedding planner and I trust her opinion. And that nail polish thing is a good idea."

"Let's leave Hal alone. I don't want her to go into her tool bag and mistakenly string me from the ceiling so people can kiss under me."

"So you're saying it's a mistle-no then?"

Sacha felt the scream well up in her throat but washed it down with another sip of coffee. A few drops spilled on the floor and disappeared into the thick blue rug. She needed to ignore the bait. Only four more days to get through and that's *if* she stayed for Christmas, a plan more doubtful every second she stayed in this dress.

Sacha looked at her bare shoulders in the mirror. The almost indecent neckline made her wish she'd packed her best pushup bra. "I don't understand how something with so little fabric can be so hot."

"I went with the velvet to keep you warm, Sach. I was thinking of you."

"Were you thinking I would want to light myself on fire in this dress?"

A soft knock on the door cut off Alexis's reply.

Hal closed the door softly behind her. There was something not entirely professional about the way Hal's eyes scanned Sacha's body in the full-length mirror. Her slow appraisal of Sacha in the green monster dress sent a little shiver through her, hot as hell velvet be damned.

Hal made eye contact with Alexis. "I got your text. What's the emergency?"

"Sacha is the emergency. Her dress doesn't fit at all."

Sacha felt Hal's gaze traveling over her body again and she caught a mumbled, "I wouldn't say not at all."

Sacha threw all of her focus behind trying not to squirm under Hal's assessment, counting the seconds off in her head. Finally, Hal nodded definitively and took a step toward her.

Hal was in a black sweater, dark skinny jeans, and black Chelsea boots that were on the rugged side of sophisticated. They were the kind of boots that a country song would say looked good under her bed, and picturing just that gave Sacha a brand-new goal to focus on. It might be her sister's wedding but there wasn't any reason she couldn't have a little fun, right? Besides, weren't single bridesmaids essentially obligated to hook up with someone at a wedding?

Hal ran her hands along Sacha's shoulders to straighten her posture and the soft brush of cashmere from Hal's sleeve against her bare skin gave her the sudden urge to nuzzle into Hal. Being back at this cabin was doing weird things to her. Sacha wasn't a cuddler, at least not in the past, but something about Hal was telegraphing comfort. Sacha focused instead on the way Hal's jeans hugged her thighs. She imagined slowly pulling them down, after divesting her of the boots, of course.

Hal cleared her throat drawing Sacha's attention, and her green eyes caught hers in the mirror. "Ready?" Hal's voice came out rough, splintered with something she wasn't saying.

"I'm ready." Sacha gestured to the mirror like a game show host showing off a grand prize. "Please fix this mess."

Hal's voice was almost a whisper as she said, "I don't see a mess."

Sacha was not prepared for Hal to kneel in front of her. Watching it happen made her knees weak. As she steadied herself, her foot caught in the hem of the dress and she stumbled forward into Hal. Hal caught her with a steadying hand on her hip. *Good reflexes*, Sacha noted. Hal's green eyes looked up into hers and Sacha licked her lips before catching herself. Flirting was fine, but she probably shouldn't devour her sister's wedding planner. At least not in front of her.

Hal unzipped the leather bag she had secured across her chest and pulled out a pin cushion and a small box of safety pins.

"What else do you have in that bag?" Sacha asked.

"What do you mean?" Hal glanced up at her.

"Well, yesterday it was tools and lipstick. And a phone charger. But today you're a mobile tailor shop."

"Oh, right, I just keep a little of everything. Always be prepared and all that."

What else was she prepared for exactly?

For the next fifteen minutes, as Hal folded and pinned fabric and studied the curves of Sacha's body, she barely breathed. Even with a handful of sharp pins, Hal was the softest thing in the room.

Hal made promises to come collect the dress in fifteen minutes and drop it off at the seamstress that afternoon.

Once the door had clicked closed, Alexis spun toward Sacha like she was on ice. She had the dress pushed down to her hips, the skin below her collar bone flushed.

"Are you alright? I guess you weren't kidding about that dress being really hot."

"Very funny. So, Hal? That was a surprise."

"Isn't she amazing? If you hadn't skipped my bachelorette party, you would have known sooner. And you'd have already tried on this dress."

"I didn't skip it—I had a work trip that was already planned and telling my client that I had to cancel to party at a casino with my sister and some male strippers wouldn't have done me any favors."

"I mean, it might have done you some favors."

A rap on the door startled both of them. Sacha tossed the dress onto the bed and slipped back into her jeans and sweater. That was a pretty quick fifteen minutes. Maybe Hal didn't have a watch in her bag.

The door swung wide open and Todd stood in the doorway.

"It's customary to wait for a response before just opening a door." Sacha crossed her arms over her chest, feeling a sudden chill now that she was no longer wrapped in velvet or Hal's attention.

Todd shrugged. "I heard you talking. Lexus, are you done here? We have people arriving soon and I think we should both be there to greet them."

"Sure thing, babe. I'll be down in a minute."

As soon as the door shut, Alexis turned on Sacha with a finger raised. "I know what you're going to say."

Sacha raised an eyebrow. "You let him call you Lexus? As in the luxury vehicle?"

"As in a cute nickname, you jerk. You know, you'd like Todd if you just gave him a chance."

"I did give him a chance. He threw a tantrum when I beat him at a lawn game."

"Okay, that was bad, but he hates to lose. It wouldn't have killed you to let him win."

"It would have, actually."

"Enough. I know he's not your favorite person, but he is mine, so please behave."

"I shall do my best. Now go greet your guests."

CHAPTER 4
HAL

The snow was falling softly, a light layer glittering in the mid-day sun like a city street after a pride parade. Hal could not have planned the day better herself. Though she had planned it, and down to the very last detail.

Todd's parents had arrived that morning along with Owen, the best man, who happened to be the worst in Hal's opinion. After making sure that they were settled at the Inn, Hal finally had time to focus on her tasks without interruption.

First item of business was to head down to the pond and make sure everyone had what they needed for ice skating. The groom's bros, as they had creatively dubbed themselves, were planning on a pickup hockey game later, but until then there would be ice skates and hot chocolate available for those without a death wish.

Hal heard Sacha's laugh before she saw her. It wasn't light and musical, Sacha's laugh had a roughness to it that meant business, like her amusement was a surprise that caught her off guard. Sacha was huddled in a gray sweater, the green beanie on her head catching snowflakes.

Hal paused, waiting for Sacha to catch up with her.

"You really outdid yourself with this snow, Hal. Even I have to admit it's lovely."

"Yeah, well, I called in a few favors to get everyone in the holiday wedding mood."

Sacha tilted her head to the side, a grin spreading across her face. "Oh, I think you're definitely getting people in the mood."

Hal's breath caught and she pulled her collar up to hide the blush creeping up her neck. It seemed a lot like Sacha Brighton was flirting with her, but years of experience told Hal that it simply didn't make sense. "So, um, are you going to skate?" *Smooth response,* Hal thought to herself.

"Probably not. I think Alexis would end me if I got all bruised before the wedding. How about you?"

"Oh, I don't think so." Hal tapped her notebook against her hand. "Too much to check off my list today."

"Oh, like what?"

"Just normal stuff. Checking the linens. Calling the florist to confirm delivery for tomorrow night. Making sure I have the right glitter pens for the guestbook."

"Glitter pens, really, that's on your list?"

Hal tapped two-thirds of the way down the page. "I'm sure they're the right ones, but I want Alexis to have a chance to test them on the guestbook paper to confirm they look exactly how she imagined."

"Wow, that's, um, detail-oriented of you."

"Of course, that's my job." Hal expected Sacha to tease her for being uptight but instead she seemed fascinated and a little impressed. Hal wasn't used to people looking at her like they wanted to know more.

"I'm just lucky if I'm wearing matching socks." Sacha looked down at her boots, her brows pulling together like she couldn't remember if her socks matched that day. "Maybe you can help me with that for the wedding."

Sacha winked at her and Hal felt a little flutter in her chest before a spike of panic crept between her ribs. "Wait, you're not wearing socks to the wedding. You'll need nylons with your dress. But I have some for you."

Sacha's hand came to rest gently on Hal's shoulder as she brought her lips close to Hal's ear. "You're too easy to rile up, Hal."

As the ice came into view, Hal saw Owen's coppery hair backlit by the sun like it was catching fire. He was skating backward, executing a complicated series of stops that sprayed ice up to his knees. Hal looked around to see who the show had been for but no one else was around.

"Hey, Sach." Owen called out and Hal felt Sacha stop beside her.

Hal felt a tug on the back of her jacket and turned to see Sacha standing behind her, trying to hide.

"What's he doing here?"

"He's Todd's best man. Are you hiding? I'm pretty sure he saw you."

"This is a nightmare. Was this Alexis's plan to set me up with someone at the wedding? I was so in love with him in high school, but he's always been way out of my league. Not to mention a bit of a jerk. It took me so long to realize that boys being mean isn't actually a sign that they like you, it's just them telling you who they really are."

"You think that guy's out of your league? He's still hitting balls off of a t, and you're in the majors."

"Why Hal, are you calling me a major babe?" Sacha batted her lashes, a move Hal never thought could be this effective.

Hal's eyes went wide. "What? No, I uh—I was just saying he's not out of your league, it's the opposite really. I'm sorry if that was inappropriate of me. I know I'm just here to help Alexis with the wedding, not offer you dating advice."

Sacha tilted her head and squinted a bit in the sun. "I wouldn't be so sure about that. And no need to be sorry. I haven't felt that good since you felt me up in my dress this morning."

Hal's complexion paled like she was trying to disappear into the snow falling around them. "Oh no, I was just—"

Sacha's laugh broke the tension between them. "Ok, I'll stop teasing you now, but you're very cute when you're embarrassed." She reached up and straightened the lapel of Hal's pea coat. "It's nice to see you a little undone."

And with that, Sacha turned on her heel, threw Owen a wave, and headed in the direction of where he'd stopped on the ice to observe their conversation.

Hal didn't know what to make of the strange feeling swirling in her stomach. A mix of attraction and something she was ashamed to admit felt a lot like a sharp stab of jealousy. She stood still, nearly holding her breath, watching Sach approach the edge of the ice, head tucked slightly, and hands shoved into her pockets. Owen skated over to her, dusting the bottom of Sacha's pants with a spray of ice from his dramatic halt. Sacha hopped back a bit, but Owen reached out, placing his hand on her upper arm to pull her closer.

Hal wished she could hear what they were saying. There must be something she could check over there anyway. She could work and eavesdrop, multitasking was the cornerstone of any good wedding planner after all, and this wasn't amateur hour. Hal made her way to the small wooden picnic table and adjusted the carafe of hot chocolate.

"Come on, Sach, just one skate."

"I really shouldn't."

"I thought you used to be fun. Maybe I'll just pull you out here and I can hold you up like old times."

Hal glanced over the hot chocolate, her mouth drawing into a tight line. She didn't like that Owen's hand was still gripping Sacha's shoulder even though she was leaning away from him, like her whole body was battling between politeness and escape.

"If you want someone to skate with so badly, I'll skate with you." Hal was surprised to hear the hoarseness in her own voice.

Sacha turned to her, her mouth falling open slightly. Hal thought for a moment of walking up and putting her arm around Sacha's shoulders, but that would make her no better than Owen. No one had a claim on Sacha, but if Hal could get this guy to leave her alone, she would.

Owen stared at Hal without responding so she took a few steps forward, standing a bit taller. "What? Am I not cute enough for you to skate with?"

Owen let go of Sacha's arm and slithered back a few strides.

"Anyone can skate if they want to. Free country and all that," he said gruffly as he continued to inch backward toward the center of the ice.

"Great, I'll grab some skates."

Sacha's breath was warm on Hal's neck as she leaned in and whispered, "you really don't have to do this."

"And he didn't need to harass you, but here we are. I'll take care of it."

"That's sweet, Hal. But I can handle Owen. He's not as tough as he looks. Actually, if I remember correctly, he has his kind moments."

Sacha's words of praise for Owen soured in Hal's stomach and only renewed her determination to knock him down a peg. She would just have to be a buffer between this buffoon and Sacha.

Hal laced up the hockey skates that happened to be close to her size and took a few tentative steps onto the ice. She bent her knees and pushed with her back leg. Surely skating was like riding a bike or at the very least like roller skating. Same mechanics and all that. She thanked her stars for her friend April, roller derby extraordinaire, who once naively thought Hal was cut out for the game and tried to teach her to skate. At least tryouts had taught her how to throw a discrete elbow here and there.

Hal took a tentative spin around then smiled at Sacha who seemed to be biting back a grin. When their eyes locked, Sacha winked at Hal and she felt a shiver of nerves and possibility run through her. Then Owen slid between them, his little spray of ice following him like a cloud of gnats.

"How about a race then?"

"Why?"

"Why not? You were so eager to skate; a little friendly competition couldn't hurt. First across the pond and back is the winner." Owen paused and pitched his voice lower. "And the loser backs off. Look, I know she's into women too, she always has been, but I think this wedding could be a real chance for us to reconnect. It's what everyone wants."

"Is Sacha part of that everyone? Because she wasn't even aware that you'd be here."

"Who cares. Sacha's never known what's best for

herself. She needs someone who can make decisions for her. Keep her in line and all that."

Hal gritted her teeth. She'd throw a hundred discrete elbows to take the wind out of his douche-y sails.

"Fine, let's go."

Owen executed a slow spin and crouched like a sprinter, so Hal followed suit.

From behind them Sacha's voice echoed out over the ice. "What are you two doing? Do not race. Alexis will be so mad if either of you get hurt."

When Hal glanced back, Sacha was picking her way to the ice, she must have put on skates during Owen's blustering. She smiled at Sacha and felt her heart do a little spin when Sacha winked at her.

"Stop staring." Owen elbowed Hal. "Ready, set—". The "go" echoed behind him as he took off. Hal took a few unsteady lunges before finding her footing and chasing after him.

Sacha called out behind her but all she could hear was the rush of her breath and the click of her blades on the frozen surface of the pond.

Hal's legs were strong beneath her as her skates sliced a clean path across the ice. Each stride leaving behind a clean white line in the mirror surface. She felt like she was flying down a hill on a sled. Suddenly something solid made contact with her chest and her entire body felt like a car stopping short. The air left her lungs in an aggressive whoosh. Hal paused, hands on her burning quads as she caught her breath.

"You can't clothesline people, Owen." Sacha's voice was a little breathless behind her.

Hal straightened and pushed off again. Focusing only

on speed. Owen's red fleece came into view and just as she pulled even with him, he threw an arm out again to block her. She ducked to avoid him, losing her footing and stumbling a bit before righting herself. She very nearly found herself up close and personal with the ice.

Hal lowered her head and kept her eyes on the flash of Owen's skates, glinting in the sun like knives. This time when she pulled even with him, *she* threw an elbow into his ribs before he realized she was there. He let out a huff of air and Hal pulled ahead, only slowing to spin for the return trip.

Sacha looked beautiful heading right toward her, dark hair flowing out from beneath her knit hat.

As Hal passed her Sacha raised a hand and wagged a finger at her. "Behave, please, before I have to show you both up."

Behind them Owen barked out a laugh. "Please Sacha, shouldn't you be cheering on the side?"

Hal heard a grunt of frustration as Sacha did a quick turn and started gaining on her and Owen. He bumped into Hal's back as he tried to pass her and knock her off balance in one go. She threw another elbow into his midsection for good measure. As Hal and Owen struggled for the lead, Sacha sailed past them with a little wave, her hair blowing behind her like a victory flag.

Sacha moved effortlessly and Hal couldn't take her eyes off her. It was like she was dancing across the ice, not battling it to stay upright.

Hal heard a loud clatter and something wrapped around her ankle. Her knee broke her fall, smacking into the surface of the ice so hard she expected it to crack beneath her; she was almost surprised she didn't see the cracks splinter out in all directions. She let out a yelp as her knee made crunching contact with the ice.

She laid there for a moment, steadying her breath and focusing on the perfect cold as she rested her cheek on the freezing cold surface. Owen's hand was still wrapped around her ankle, keeping her from sitting up and assessing the damage.

Hal propped herself on one elbow and looked at Owen, where he was sprawled across the ice like he was doing an army crawl. "You've already taken me down. Can you let go of me now?" Hal blinked back the tears in her eyes. She wouldn't willingly give him the satisfaction. To his credit, Owen also looked a bit dazed.

Hal tried to press up onto her knees but the pain that emanated from her right leg was incredible and overwhelming. She gingerly brought her hand to her knee and her palm came away sticky with blood. Well, that couldn't be a good sign. How was she going to get everything done if she couldn't even walk? How could Hal have lost focus on the task she was here to do? She was here to help Alexis and make her wedding perfect, not act like some knight jousting for Sacha's favor like she was some maiden to be won.

Sacha slid to a stop and bent down on one knee beside Hal. "I see Owen was so busy staring at me that he tripped over his own feet."

"If you didn't want people to stare, you shouldn't wear jeans like that," Owen called out.

"You're gross and wrong. What a terrible combination!" Sacha said over her shoulder with mock cheer.

"Are you ok, Hal? I told you not to race him." Sacha placed a hand on her shoulder, her other hand hovered above Hal's knee like she was casting a spell.

"Yeah, I'm ok. And I would have been fine if he didn't drag me down."

"Well, mostly fine."

"What do you mean?"

"I assume your pride would have been a little bruised by how easily I smoked you both." Sacha's grin took the sting out of her statement. "Do you want me to call an ambulance? Get you a sled?"

"No, really, I'm ok. I can get up." Hal grimaced as she shifted on the ice.

"Here, I'll help you."

Sacha slid her hand into Hal's, her fingers cool against Hal's warm palm. Hal jerked her hand away and then held her bloody palm up as a way of explanation. Sacha's brow wrinkled, but she reached for Hal's hand again.

"Just a bruise, huh? I don't like the look of that blood. We need to get you inside and cleaned up."

With surprising ease, Sacha pulled Hal to her feet. She barely had time to wonder at Sacha's strength because the second Hal put weight on her knee she collapsed again. She was saved from another bone-crushing fall only by Sacha pulling her forward into a hug to hold her up. The pain was intense, but the warmth of Sacha's body pressed to hers felt worth it. The wind picked up and Sacha's hair brushed against her face and filled Hal's senses with its subtle scent of ginger.

"Do you think you can skate if I hold you up? Just lift your hurt leg off the ice."

And so, Hal found herself being pulled across the ice, hand in hand with Sacha who skated backward and held eye contact with her. Sacha asked if Hal was okay every time she so much as winced.

Sacha's grip tightened and she pulled Hal a little closer. "Close your eyes if you need to, I've got you."

Hal closed her eyes. The pain in her knee was overwhelmed by the nearness of Sacha. And this feeling of being cared for that was like a rising sun in her chest. If this was as close to romance as she could get with Sacha Brighton, she'd take it.

CHAPTER 5
SACHA

Sacha skated backward with delicate care that she wasn't aware she possessed. She clasped Hal's hands softly.

"What about me?" Owen called out from where he lay on the ice. He'd somehow found a reserve of survival adrenaline and managed to turn over and prop his arms under his head, bathing in the sun's rays like a satisfied cat.

Sacha laughed to herself. It turned out Owen was just as annoying as ever. But she'd seen something intriguing in Hal. Chivalry she could have predicted, but fierce competitiveness she wouldn't have.

"It seems like you can manage," Sacha called before she returned her focus to Hal, who was looking down at their feet.

They reached the edge of the lake and she spun Hal around and held her hands as she sat down on the small bank of snow. Hal leaned forward to untie her skates but the groan she let out was pitiful.

Sacha put her hand on Hal's shoulder and pressed

gently until Hal relaxed. "Just wait here. And don't try to do anything until I'm back."

She retrieved their boots and quickly removed her own skates. When she returned, Hal was still leaning back on her hands, wearing sunglasses she hadn't had a minute ago.

"Where did you get those?"

Hal lowered her glasses a bit. "I always keep a pair of sunglasses in my bag."

"The Sleigh really has everything, doesn't it?"

"The Sleigh?"

"Yeah, that magic bag you carry with you everywhere. Somehow you've fit every possible need into an impossibly small space. You're like Santa on Christmas Eve with his magical sleigh full of presents."

Hal shrugged. "It has a lot of pockets; the trick is keeping it all organized."

"I don't suppose you have any anti-inflammatories in there?"

"I do, but those are for emergencies."

"And what would you call this?" Sacha knelt and lifted Hal's ankle to loosen the laces of her skate, but the knot didn't budge.

"They're for other people's emergencies. I have some other pain meds in the first aid kit in my trunk."

"Of course you do." Sacha tried again to untie Hal's skate, but between her cold fingers and the bondage-level knot, she was not making progress. "What kind of knot is this? It's impossible."

"Oh, I don't know if it has a name. I always triple knot my laces. I didn't want them to come undone and risk falling. A little moot now, I guess."

"Leave it to you to use a bespoke shoelace knot." At last, Sacha undid the knot and loosened the laces, sliding Hal's foot from the skate. Her socks looked like Christmas sweaters, navy blue covered in snowflakes and pine trees. "You're really into Christmas, huh?"

"Well, I have spent several months planning a Christmas Eve wedding. If I wasn't in the spirit by now, I'd be in trouble. Do you not like Christmas?"

"I enjoy having a few days off from work. And eating takeout."

"Sounds like a challenge."

"Ask anyone, Challenge is my middle name."

Hal squinted at Sacha, but seemed to decide against saying anything else. Sacha finished putting Hal's boots back on but left them untied.

"I'll need to fix these if I'm going to walk to the house."

"Good thing you're not going to walk to the house. You could barely even stand." Sacha leaned into Hal. She resisted the urge to smooth Hal's short dark hair back into place as she slipped one arm under Hal's legs.

"I promise I can walk." Hal hobbled to a standing position, balancing on the toe of her hurt leg.

"Do you ever accept help?" Sacha took a step toward Hal.

"I'm not sure I've ever really needed it."

"Interesting. You're going to be in quite the predicament for the next few days then. Ok, ready? You better hold on unless you want me to drop you."

Hal grumbled but wrapped her arms around Sacha's neck. Sacha drew in a deep breath and focused on appearing at ease as she bent her knees and lifted Hal. It wasn't easy, but it was hard to ignore how nice Hal felt in her arms as she swept her off her feet and walked toward the house.

Hal shot Owen a grin and a little wave before resting

her head on Sacha's shoulder. "Something about this feels backward." Her voice buzzed against Sacha's neck and she had to suppress a shiver.

"Yeah? Well, you should probably get used to it."

THE HOUSE WAS quiet as Sacha carried Hal over the threshold and lowered her onto the leather couch in the den.

"Where's Alexis?"

"She was getting her hair colored and then she and your mom had a spa appointment."

Sacha felt the sting of disappointment. The event sounded terrible, but it still would have been nice to have been asked.

Hal reached up from where she lay prone on the couch. "They didn't think you'd want to go."

"And they were right!" Sacha forced the cheer into her voice and turned away quickly, searching the room for something to bring Hal. She settled on a pillow to go under her knee.

"Thanks." Hal leaned back onto the couch.

"Not so fast there, cowboy. Why don't you take off your pants and tell me what you need?"

Hal's eyes widened as Sacha replayed the last few seconds in her head.

"Oh god, I just heard how that sounded. I meant take your pants off so I can check your knee."

"That's ok. It's fine."

"Great, then it's not an issue for me to check."

Hal stood unsteadily and slid down her pants. Sacha pretended very hard that she wasn't admiring Hal's boxer briefs which were black and covered with snowflakes.

Sacha knelt in front of Hal and softly placed her hand behind Hal's knee to lift it slightly. Hal's hand found her head and then slipped to her shoulder for balance. Sacha felt a tightness in her stomach. *Relax, Brighton. She's hurt, this position is probably lost on her.*

Hal shivered. "Sorry, your fingers are a little cold."

"Oh, sorry." Sacha blew warm air on the fingers of her other hand. Hal froze, only taking a breath when Sacha switched her hands and focused on the cut on her knee. *So maybe this position isn't lost on her.*

"No, it's... thanks for doing this." Hal's voice had a slight catch to it.

"Ok, you're right about the bruise. Do you have anything I can use to clean the cut and bandage it in your magic bag, or should I go scavenge?"

"I've got it covered, thanks." Hal straightened and let go of Sacha's shoulder as she reached for her bag.

"Okay." Sacha felt suddenly desperate to kiss Hal, to push her back on the couch and have a good old fashioned high school make out session... which would be inappropriate. Probably. Given the circumstances. She clasped her hands behind her back as Hal put antibacterial gel on her cut. "I'm going to grab you some ice. Is there anything else you need?"

"My computer, maybe? It's in the room where I'm staying. In my bag. I might as well get some work done."

"Or you could take a day off to recover and be super productive tomorrow?"

"I think ice skating put me—" Hal paused and glanced at her watch, "—47 minutes behind schedule."

"O-kay, so you're one of those people."

Hal raised an eyebrow and popped the pills into her mouth followed by a gulp of water. "Say more."

"A down-to-the-minute scheduler."

"Of course. Is there any other way to get through the day?"

"I'll be back in a few. And against my better judgment I will get your computer from your room. Please rest for the next 2.7 minutes."

Hal's chuckle followed her as she made her way up the stairs.

Sacha was pretty sure she was in the room where Hal was staying, though there was no clear sign of anyone staying there at all. The bed was neatly made. There were no clothes or towels on the floor. No water glass on the nightstand or phone charger strung across the floor like a tripwire. Leave it to Hal to give her absolutely no opportunity to snoop respectfully.

She spotted a leather bag, roughly the size of a computer, tucked away neatly next to the trunk at the foot of the bed. Sacha thought about going through it but didn't want to invade Hal's privacy. Well, obviously she did, but she was hoping for a chance to view things in the open, like looking at a museum exhibit. Opening the bag felt more like breaking and entering. She hoisted it onto her shoulder and shut the door behind her.

HAL WAS LAYING down when she returned, and she opened her eyes at Sacha's approach. Sacha felt a mix of relief and disappointment to see Hal's festive underwear were no longer on display.

"I was hoping you'd maybe fallen asleep."

Hal squinted at her. "I'm not much of a napper. Too much to do."

"Of course." Sacha laid out the satchel on the coffee table and handed Hal the glass of water. "I hate to break it to you, Hal, but you're going to have to use your emergency pain meds from your magic bag unless you want to give me the keys to your car or permission to ransack your room."

Hal grumbled but pulled the ibuprofen from a pocket inside her bag.

"Ok, take those. I'm going to prop your knee up on a pillow so we can ice it." Sacha pulled one of the fluffy white pillows from the far end of the couch.

"Wait, can you check to make sure I don't have anything on my pants?"

Sacha raised an eyebrow at Hal. Why was she worried about that now? Should she have checked her for a concussion? And is that something Siri could tell her how to do?

"I don't want to get mud or anything on the pillow."

"Oh, we'll just wash it."

Hal reached forward and brushed her fingers over the pillow, making the slightest contact with Sacha's hand. "It's alpaca, I think. So, I'd have to get it dry cleaned."

"Or we throw it out and they never notice. It looks like they hunted the abominable snowman to make this."

Hal looked so shocked that Sacha laughed. "Taste aside, that pillow probably cost a few hundred dollars."

"Fine, so we say I spilled something on it, and I promise to replace it and then I forget."

"That is *a* plan. *Or* you could check to see if I have mud on my pants?"

"But the ground is covered in snow. And you fell on the ice."

"Better safe than sorry."

"Fine, turn over and let me see."

Hal rolled to one side and Sacha felt proud of the quick and respectful amount of time she checked out her ass before scanning the rest of her pants. Truly, her restraint deserved a medal.

"Perfect. Ah, I mean perfectly clean, just as I suspected." Sacha helped Hal roll back over, touching her hip for just a moment before realizing what she was doing. She probably shouldn't make a move on the hot but injured wedding planner, right? Her relationship with her sister was already rocky enough. "No absurd pillows will be ruined today. Happy now?"

"Mmhmm, very. I'll take the ice now."

"How about you rest and let me finish up?"

Hal leaned back on the couch and pulled a small note-book from her bag and checked something off.

"What are you checking off?"

"Hot chocolate for ice skating." Hal flipped to a new page and studied it.

"So those are all your to-do lists."

"Well, some of them. This one's guests."

"You really are like Santa with your list of names. Is that your naughty list or your nice one?"

"Well, the first name on it is Grandma Shirley, so I'm hoping for nice."

"Oh my god Grams is coming? She's so mean to everyone. You'll love her."

Hal laughed. "Yeah, she sounds great."

"Oh, she is. She hates every gift I give her, and I'm her absolute favorite person. Just imagine how she eviscerates everyone else."

Hal continued to study her list. She bit the end of her pen, eyes narrowing at the page in concentration.

"Well, I'll let you focus for a bit. Just call out if you need anything." Sacha draped a blanket over Hal and headed out of the room.

SACHA HEARD Hal's voice and practically teleported back to the den. But Hal was huddled under the blue and white plaid blanket mumbling. Her usually artfully disheveled hair was disheveled in earnest and Sacha surprised herself by running her fingers through it, smoothing back the soft strands. Hal said something unintelligible and turned over, pulling the blanket over her head. The soft thud of her notebook hitting the floor drew Sacha's attention. Its leather cover was soft beneath her fingers and its well-loved pages fell open to the crimson ribbon marking today's tasks.

There were a host of tasks already checked off, including perfect hot chocolate and set up ice skating. Next item on the list: bride and groom gingerbread cookies. Alexis's favorite cookies. Sacha vaguely remembered making them once or twice when they had sleepovers at their Grams' house. She took a deep breath, gently closed the notebook, and tucked it back into Hal's Sleigh Bag. There was no use in Hal being stressed about losing the day. Sacha could definitely handle making a few cookies.

THE KITCHEN WAS CAVERNOUS, and with all the tile and marble, the acoustics were amazing. Pristine copper pots hung over the marble island, as flawless as the day they were forged. Sacha couldn't remember the last time she'd been in this kitchen. Growing up, neither of her parents had cooked and *certainly* not on vacation. Sacha seemed to remember them being on vacation more often than not. She spent a while digging through cabinets looking for a mixing bowl. All she could find was a white ceramic bowl with an intricate raised design that reminded her of paisley.

All she had to do was mix some ingredients and bake them. How hard could it possibly be?

Sacha pulled her phone out of her pocket and searched for a gingerbread cookie recipe. Step one, she thought to herself, then laughed. She'd only been around Hal two days and already she was thinking in steps. If she started making lists, she'd seek help. The recipe seemed basic enough filled with the usual suspects: flour, butter, eggs. Molasses might be an issue, but surely Hal had gotten everything she'd need.

She thought about putting music on but settled for humming to herself, so she didn't wake Hal.

Sacha opened the fridge. The bright light shone against the pristine interior like the sun bouncing off the snow. The shelves were blinding and empty as a frozen tundra. In the door, a single carton of soy milk sat next to a few yogurts. Alexis. She grabbed the soy milk and headed to the pantry, gathering the ceramic canisters of flour and sugar. A glass bottle of molasses was sitting on a low shelf, and she tucked it into the crook of her arm like a newborn.

A new search for vegan gingerbread cookies led her to a blog where she had to endure a woman named Sally's entire life story just to find out what to substitute for an egg. She felt very close to giving up and taking a nap with Hal instead. Sacha scavenged an admittedly pitiful banana she had in her room from breakfast. Her survival skills were at full throttle. Sacha picked the cinnamon and nutmeg from the decorative spice rack, peeling off the safety labels as she went. All Spice was nowhere to be found. She doubled the other spices. Close enough.

The mixer sent the flour into the air like a grenade, so she settled for hand mixing all the ingredients together, carefully following Sally's narrative about the one time her husband missed his flight to see her for the holidays and she made a batch of these cookies and drove 1,000 miles in a blizzard to deliver them.

The dough was wet and sticky and quite unpleasant, which was perfect according to Sally's 48 progress pictures. She slid the bowl of cookie dough into the empty fridge to chill for the 30 minutes Sally recommended as the exact perfect amount of time for fabulous cookies you'd be willing to drive through a blizzard for. Marriage material cookies.

Sacha studied herself. Her jeans looked like she'd walked through a dust storm and she was barely half done. What had she been thinking when she decided to make cookies for the wedding? Sacha didn't even like Todd. And it wasn't for Alexis, not really. She thought of Hal sleeping on the couch and the stressed look she'd had on her face when she'd checked her list. So, this was what, helping out a friend? A friend who just happens to be kind and attractive and absolutely clobbered your ex in a skate race earlier? Sure, it's good to have friends.

She sprinkled flour on the marble surface of the island and rolled out the dough with a matching marble rolling pin that surely required a heavy machinery license to operate. Not one of the 111 drawers in the kitchen held a cookie-cutter. Perhaps the perfect Hal had forgotten this crucial detail? Sacha thought about looking in the Sleigh Bag—is a cookie-cutter something Hal would keep in that bag? And would a mere mortal like her opening the bag somehow drain its magic?

She settled on a paring knife and carefully cut out approximations of people. She made them all bride shapes, partly because gender roles were a construct and partly because she kept messing up the legs and the skirt of a gown was significantly less work.

Sacha checked on Hal and confirmed she was still asleep as the first batch baked. The alarmist beep of the oven timer broke her focus. She hit the button to make it stop, but it kept going, and when she opened the oven, the smell of burnt sugar hit her full-on. Not the timer then, the smoke alarm. She stripped off her sweater and waved it at the ceiling until the beeping stopped. The cookies had baked for less than ten minutes but were singed beyond salvation. She turned off the oven to let it cool and emptied the baking sheet into the trash.

The second batch turned out very close to edible, and she spent her time carefully decorating them with the icing she'd made out of confectioners' sugar. She even mimicked a lace bodice that Alexis had mentioned her dress had. At the very least, these cookies would *look* incredible.

Somehow this entire process had taken several hours. Headlights sliced through the perfect darkness of 5 pm startling her. At least she could show Alexis the cookies.

The back door creaked open and a raspy voice that was decidedly not Alexis cut through the silence. "I can't believe you'd let an old woman struggle with her own luggage."

Sacha rushed to the door and took the tote bag from her grandma's hand. "This is your luggage?"

"No, my luggage is waiting for you in the car, my love. I said I can't believe you'd let me struggle with it and I know you won't." The old woman punctuated her statement by tapping Sacha's nose with a crooked index finger. She looked around the kitchen. "Have you been baking unsupervised? You look a mess."

Sacha widened her eyes and nodded. "I was making gingerbread cookies for the rehearsal after-party tomorrow."

"Alexis's favorite. Did you poison them?"

"Not intentionally. But I did make only brides."

"Very mature of you. Todd is probably too masculine to eat cookies. He told me once he doesn't wear shoes without laces because those are for girls. Can you imagine tying all those bows?" Grams laughed. "Now go get my bags so I can give you your gift in secret."

As Sacha unwrapped and quickly put on the handmade grey cable-knit sweater, which she would now pretend she always had, Grams headed over to inspect the cookies.

"Did you make brides or abominable snowmen?" She held up a cookie and some of the white icing dripped onto her fingers. They were decidedly monstrous. Grams set the cookie down and tasted the icing on her finger before grabbing a paper towel. "Come here."

Sacha leaned in and Grams reached toward her face with a glint in her eye. Instead of wiping away the flour that was on her face Grams traced a heart like she was drawing on a dirty car window.

"Thanks for that, Grams." Sacha reached to wipe off her face.

"Don't ruin it. I've actually improved the situation. You look darling. A beautiful disaster." Grams winked at Sacha.

"I'm very good at making mistakes."

"I think mistakes while trying hard might be your love language. Alexis put you on cookie duty? What's she busy doing?"

"Spa appointment with mom. And she didn't put me up to it. I was just trying to help."

Grams narrowed her eyes. "Do you remember the time I gave you my family recipe book for your birthday?"

"Yes, I keep it in my safe."

"Do you remember what you told me when you unwrapped it before anyone arrived?"

Sacha shook her head. She loved hearing about past versions of herself from Grams. It was like watching an old movie she'd forgotten she loved.

"You said, 'Grams, the only thing I'm ever going to bake is toast.'"

Sacha laughed. "Oh, right! That was the day you explained to me how toast is made."

"Do you think these are better or worse than your toast?"

Well, she'd tried. "I know they look bad because they were maybe a little bit warm when I put the icing on. But at least I got a picture of how beautiful I made the dresses!" Sacha pulled up her photos, she'd used a toothpick to get the detailing on the bodice.

"Those, my dear, are beautiful. Next time, we've got to work on your process instead of rushing to the art."

"Maybe they taste good? I followed a recipe. Well, I loosely followed a modified vegan recipe." Sacha closed one eye as Grams bit off the head of the bride of Frankenstein. She heard the snap of the decapitation from across the kitchen followed by a cough.

"It's like a jawbreaker if jawbreakers were too salty. I thought you said you *didn't* poison them."

Sacha bit back a laugh. "I had some trouble with the oven."

"Your mother with this damn fancy convection oven that she had to have but never uses. I have a hard time using them too because the timing and temperature are different.

Just because something's the most expensive doesn't make it better."

Had Sacha known it was a convection oven? She had not. Though it probably wouldn't have made much of a difference. "Right, let's blame mom and the oven."

Grams winked at Sacha. "Works for me."

CHAPTER 6
HAL

Hal raised herself onto her elbows. All the light had left the sky while she slept. She grabbed her phone to check the time, panic thrumming in her chest like a game show countdown. She'd gotten barely a third of her to-do list done today. All those lonely items without their check marks sent a stab of guilt through her chest. How could she have let Alexis down like that? Maybe if she got up now and rushed, she could check a few more things off.

She rose to her feet, her knee buckling just slightly before begrudgingly supporting her. Sacha's laugh cracking through the air drew her attention, and a smile pulled at the corners of her mouth. Sacha carrying her to the house earlier like a bride on her wedding night flashed through Hal's mind and a heat rushed to her face that had nothing to do with embarrassment.

Hal shook off the feeling—she was here to work and besides, Sacha wasn't interested in her, never had been. She probably flirted with everyone, but that's all it was, empty words. Still, she couldn't stop herself from walking to the kitchen to find out what was bringing Sacha so much joy.

· · ·

THE KITCHEN LOOKED like a blizzard had hit it. Footprints tracked through the flour that dusted the floor like snow. The marble counters were hard to make out beneath the bowls and icing. Hal's fingers itched to clean up the mess, but then Sacha laughed again. She had her arm around an older woman who could only be her grandma.

The woman noticed Hal first and cleared her throat.

Sacha smiled at her. "I hope we didn't wake you up! How are you feeling?"

"I'm ok." Hal bit back the grimace as she leaned some of her weight against the doorframe.

"What's your name, dear?"

"I'm Hal, the—"

"Sacha baby, you didn't tell me you brought a beau with you."

"Grams," Sacha groaned. "Hal is helping Alexis with her wedding."

Watching Sacha squirm was quite enjoyable. Hal watched the pink bloom on her cheeks.

Grams shot Sacha a sly smile. "Now I see why you were in the mood to bake cookies. That one's enough to get anyone in the spirit."

Sacha widened her eyes and shook her head at her grandma. The pair was adorable.

"If you don't like what I have to say, my love, you can cover your ears."

"I will not cover my ears. I'm an adult." Sacha crossed her arms. Hal bit back a laugh at Sacha's pout.

Sacha's grandma gave her a stare serious enough to negotiate a nuclear arms deal.

"But if you're going to continue, I will go to my room. Don't tell any of my secrets."

"I'm just teasing you, Sachy. You couldn't keep your own secrets if I paid you to." She turned toward Hal. "Now tell me, Hal, what's the back-up plan for the cookies?"

Hal looked toward Sacha. "You made cookies? Was that the smoke alarm I heard go off earlier? I thought it was a siren in my dream."

Sacha glanced toward the trash and bit her lip. "Nope, I don't think so. No disasters here. Well, besides the mess. I saw gingerbread cookies on your list so I thought I would help while you slept."

"You should show her the pictures you took of how you decorated them, Sach," Grams said. She turned to Hal. "They were really beautiful. Did you know Sacha's an artist?"

"I'm a graphic designer, Grams." Sacha shook her head but still pulled her phone from her back pocket.

Hal stepped next to Sacha, their arms brushing as they looked at the photos. Sacha smelled like vanilla and cinnamon. Hal's stomach growled as she studied the screen. It must have taken her forever to get the icing like that, each cookie covered in an intricate pattern as delicate as a spider's web. The shattered glass of Sacha's phone actually added a nice effect.

"Those are really beautiful, Sacha. The icing is so delicate, it really looks like a lace wedding gown."

"Well, it *did* look like a lace gown." Sacha laughed. "Now it looks like a snowman that's becoming a puddle."

"Still, this is stunning. Much more beautiful than anything I could have made. Or even dreamed up. Will you send these to me?"

Sacha's cheeks flushed. She quickly shoved her phone back in her pocket. "Sure, I can send them to you later."

"And to me, too," Grams said. "I need to update my Sacha scrapbook."

The back door swung open, and a cold gust of wind brought Alexis into the kitchen. "Grams! I thought that was you when I saw the boat of a Buick parked outside."

"They just don't make cars like they used to." Grams stepped into Alexis's hug, rising onto her tiptoes.

"Who made cookies?" Alexis asked.

"Um—" Hal stammered, not sure what to say. The thought of Sacha making the cookies, something she didn't seem to enjoy, had shifted something in Hal, like a key turning a lock. She hesitated, wanting to hold that knowledge close. To protect Sacha, but from what she wasn't sure.

Alexis pinched a cookie from the tray with her long silver and blue nails.

"Well, those look crispy. Why do they look like ghosts? Hal, you probably should still get the ones from the bakery."

Hal's stomach dropped. Oh, right, *that's* what she needed to protect Sacha from. She braced herself as she looked at Sacha. She'd spent her entire afternoon trying to perfect cookies that Hal had only intended to get from the bakery. She waited for Sacha's frustration. But Sacha didn't storm off. Instead, she threw back her head and laughed.

"I'm glad there's a back-up plan because I really messed these up. And this was the better batch." Sacha wiped a tear away from her eye.

"They're truly terrible," Alexis said laughing.

"I think the cookies you used to make me out of play-doh were better. You'll probably want some water after that."

Unsure if she should excuse herself to let them enjoy their time together, Hal took a step forward tentatively. "Can I try one?"

"If we had to endure Sacha's baking, then so do you." Grams reached out for Hal's hand.

"Stop picking on me!" Sacha said with a laugh. "It's not my fault there were no ingredients in the house. It seems like there's always food here until I need to make something. Where did breakfast come from?"

"I ordered it," Hal said, glancing at her phone and swiping away a notification.

"Oh."

Hal could feel Sacha's eyes on her as she took a bite of a cookie and tried not to cough. "These are really terrible. But it means so much to me that you made them while I slept."

Sacha shoved her hands into her pockets. "It's no big deal. I didn't even need to make them."

Alexis put an arm around Sacha's shoulders. "It's the thought that counts, Sach. And these are seared into our memories forever." She pinched a bit of the sweater. "This sweater is nice. Is it new?"

"What, this?" Sacha looked down at her sweater like she was surprised to see it. "No, I've been wearing this all day."

"Wasn't your sweater earlier more of a speckled grey?" Hal wanted to pull the words back into her mouth.

Sacha caught her eye and looked like she wanted to say something, but she didn't.

Alexis sighed. "Fine, don't tell me where you got it. But at least explain what you did that has Hal limping."

Sacha went bright red. "There was a slight skating accident. Totally not my fault. If anyone's to blame, it's Owen."

"Ugh, he is a brute. Are you okay, Hal?"

Hal nodded. "Yeah, it's just a bruise and Sacha took good care of me."

"Well, that's a pleasant turn of events."

"Anyway," Sacha said loudly. "Where's mom? I thought you spent the day with her."

"She didn't have time to come in. She and dad have a party to go tonight."

"I've been here for two days and I haven't seen either of them."

"Welcome to the club, babe. Hal scheduled the spa appointment for us. Otherwise, I'm not sure I would have seen her either." Alexis forced some cheer into her voice. "I'm sure if you just call to set something up, they'll fit you in, Sach. Plus, they'll be here tomorrow for the rehearsal."

Hal felt a pang in her chest as she watched Sacha's face fall before she pinched it into a smile.

"Wow the warmth of that statement, Alexis. I feel like I need to open a window in here."

Alexis rolled her eyes. "You know how they are, Sach. If it's not benefitting them or a networking opportunity, they're really not interested. Did I tell you mom tried to get me to invite the head of a board she's trying to get a seat on to the wedding?

"Well, that sounds like the mom I know. I'm sorry, Alexis. I can help if you need anything."

"Thanks." Alexis shrugged but she blinked rapidly, her eyes wet. "It is what it is and all that. Now, who wants salad for dinner," she said with a clap.

Hal took a step toward Sacha. Her knee was protesting from standing for so long. "I'm going to sit down. I scheduled a pizza order earlier and just got the notification that's it on the way." She turned toward the table and felt Sacha's arm wrap around her.

"From Gino's?" Sacha looked at her hopefully.

"Of course."

"You're a saint. Let's get you a seat and I'll grab some more ice for that knee." Sacha's whisper sent a shiver through Hal and she wasn't sure she'd need the ice at all.

CHAPTER 7
SACHA

The ice beneath Sacha's skates made a menacing whoosh like a knife being sharpened. She crouched as she pulled into a turn, letting her fingertips brush the ice.

She'd been skating for nearly an hour, shedding layers as she went. Sacha had thrown her hat and scarf and sweater randomly onto the snow that surrounded the frozen pond. It wasn't like her to be up so early, let alone be outside doing something that was dangerously close to exercise. Her ex had called her a slow boil because she needed two hours between the time she woke up and the time she was ready to speak to another human.

But her night had been restless. She kept turning over the day before, trying to work out why she made the cookies for Alexis. Which she'd really made for Hal, if she was being honest. There was something about Hal that kept her looping in Sacha's mind, like a song she wanted to listen to with her eyes closed. When she'd arrived at the cabin a few days ago, filled with dread, Hal had seemed like a shiny thing she could distract herself with. Maybe because Hal was wrapped in lights when they met. Or maybe because Sacha didn't take anything, including herself, very seriously.

It's not that she wasn't a caring person. She was—with the right person. Or she had the potential to be. But it often took months or years for her to get to that place. Sacha felt like she'd had all that and longer with Hal. Maybe it was the familiar setting of her family's cabin or the Christmas nostalgia, or maybe it was just... Hal.

She took another lap, pushing her legs until they burned and all she could focus on was the burning in her lungs and the freezing air hitting her face. It had taken everything she had not to check on Hal throughout the night. Skating was killing time until her caring went from creepy to kind.

THE CABIN WAS ROASTING. Warm air hit her like a solid wall the moment she stepped inside. Sacha grabbed a donut from a spread laid out on the credenza. Was Hal up or did she really just have all the food scheduled?

Alexis walked into the room holding a mug of coffee. Sacha scanned the food again but didn't see any coffee.

"I don't know how you can eat that after exercising." Alexis shuddered dramatically. Was there ever a shudder that wasn't dramatic?

Sacha took a big bite of the donut, powdered sugar cascading to the wooden floor like fresh snow. "I wasn't exercising Alexis; I was having fun."

"Still talking with your mouth full, I see."

Alexis was so easy to tease it almost wasn't fair, and yet she couldn't stop herself. It seemed misguided to ruin a 29-year-streak in the name of propriety. Sacha took another big bite of her donut and grinned at Alexis.

"You look like a third-rate Santa with all that powdered sugar on your face."

"I thought you wanted me to be more festive, Lexus."

"I know you hate that name, but I like it, so joke's on you."

"Okay, Audi. Where did you get that coffee?"

"Hal has to make it."

"Why would Hal have to make the coffee."

"She's the only one who can use the espresso machine."

"Or you just didn't feel like figuring it out and so you put it on Hal?"

Sacha headed to the kitchen with Alexis on her heels. "It's a professional grade Italian machine, Sach, not a Mr. Coffee or whatever. There are knobs and settings and stuff."

"I'm pretty sure I can handle making a cup of coffee without needing Hal to rescue me."

Sacha ran her hand under cold water to take away the sting of the burn as Hal finished making her coffee. Who knew all the metal parts would get so hot? It was embarrassing to be bested by an espresso machine, but Hal speed hobbling into the kitchen after Sacha burnt herself and yelled very nearly made up for any embarrassment.

"Here you go."

Sacha took the mug from Hal as Alexis laughed from her perch on the counter. "I told you only Hal can make it."

Grams came into view over Alexis's shoulder, padding into the room in her periwinkle house coat and matching slippers.

"Do you want me to make you some coffee?" Hal asked.

Grams smiled. "No, dear. Why don't you stop taking care of these two and go get ready? I'd guess you have a lot to do today with the rehearsal tonight. I'll see if I can rustle you up a helper." Grams winked at Hal.

Sacha, Alexis, and Hal watched in half-stunned silence as Grams took a mug from the hook, approached the machine, and had it dispensing espresso in seconds.

Hal nodded once and left the room with a small smirk on her face.

Sacha grabbed her coffee and moved to follow Hal out of the room, desperate for a shower after her skating session. Grams put a hand on her arm to stop her.

"What are your plans for the day, my dear? Will you be helping Alexis or Hal?"

"Neither? I was going to do a little work before the rehearsal. I have this one client that is finding issues with every logo option I send him."

"Well, that doesn't sound worth your time. I'm sure your sister would love your help."

Sacha held back her sigh. Alexis had never once needed her help, let alone loved it.

Sacha sent Alexis a pleading look. "I don't think anyone wants my help after how those cookies turned out yesterday."

"You know I love you, dear, but sometimes I suspect you're bad on purpose because you're afraid to try and fail."

"That's a pretty harsh assessment for so early in the morning, Grams."

Grams gave Sacha's arm a gentle pat. "Then you should try waking up earlier. I've been up since 4 am. It's basically mid-day for me."

Alexis had been quietly drinking her coffee, swinging her legs back and forth as she observed the scene from her seat on the counter. Her slippers were making a sharp tapping noise where they struck the cabinets.

"Alexis, do your slippers have heels?"

"Only small ones, like kitten heels. They're very practical."

They were, in fact, the world's most impractical slippers. Silk slip ons with a fur lining. Sacha glanced down at her own mismatched socks, wishing she'd thought to pack her slippers. Hers were more of a moccasin with a rubber bottom that may or may not have doubled as her just-running-to-the-store-for-a-few-things footwear.

"Ok, ok," Sacha said. "Alexis, what help do you need today? And when are your friends getting here?"

"They're not."

"What do you mean they're not? How can they be in the wedding if they miss the rehearsal?"

"They all dropped out of the wedding, Sach. They said they couldn't miss Christmas and that I was asking too much."

"Asking too much? Are you kidding me? Didn't you *fly to Jamaica* to look at wedding venues with Amy when you were her maid of honor?"

Alexis nodded but kept her eyes trained on her coffee. She was blinking rapidly, and her cheeks were getting the telltale splotches both sisters got when they were fighting tears.

"Sorry, I don't mean to be judgmental."

"Yes, you do."

"Fine, but only because you deserve better. What can I do to help you today?"

"Not much, actually. Hal's been taking care of everything, really."

"What about mom?"

"You know how she is, Sach. As soon as she realized I

wasn't having the huge social event of the season wedding she wanted, she got too busy to help."

Grams cleared her throat. "I've got an idea. It sounds like Sacha should spend some time helping Hal today. And Alexis and I can spend the day relaxing."

"Why can't I spend the day relaxing, too?" Sacha put on her best pleading look but broke into a laugh when she caught her grandma's eye.

"Because you, my dear, are making up for lost time."

Sacha's hair was still wet from her shower when she knocked on Hal's door.

"Just a minute," Hal called out, sounding a little distressed. "Ok, come in."

Sacha eased the door open to find Hal sitting on her bed digging through her bag.

"What are you looking for?"

"More pain meds. I need to stand all day and my knee's still sore."

Sacha grimaced. "Sorry about that. But I think I know where to get some; don't move."

Sacha returned a few minutes later with a bottle of ibuprofen and a glass of water and handed both to Hal. "Maybe you can put the bottle in your magic bag, in case you need some later?"

"Good idea. I keep meaning to go to my Jeep to replenish all my supplies before the big day."

"What all do you keep in The Sleigh?"

Hal laughed. "I love that you call it that. I can't believe I never thought to name it. I keep a little of everything, I guess. I have a list."

"You have a list? Like what? An inventory?

Hal nodded.

"Can I see it?"

"No." Hal pulled her bag to her chest, holding it close.

"Fine, then I'll just guess. Do you keep duct tape in there?"

"A little. Wait are you teasing me?"

"*Moi?* I would never."

"Fine. I keep a few kinds of tape."

"What other kind?"

Hal lowered her voice to such a whisper that Sacha couldn't catch what she said.

"I didn't catch that."

With a sigh, Hal unzipped her bag and pulled out her small black notebook, flipping through the pages until she found what she was looking for.

Sacha leaned forward, trying to read the precise upside-down handwriting, but Hal shielded the list from view. "Promise you won't tease me?"

"Yes. Now gimme, please." Sacha held out her hand. Finally, Hal tentatively passed the notebook to her. She scanned the list.

"You really keep boob tape on you at all times?"

"Yup, everyone should. You never know when that kind of emergency might arise, and you definitely don't want to be unprepared."

Along with boob tape, Hal stocked a variety of items to rival any bodega including a box cutter, sewing kit, safety pins, bandages, tampons, bobby pins, a phone charger, lipstick, and super glue. It was a mix between a hardware store and a Sephora.

"That's a lot of stuff, Hal."

"There's a second page."

Sacha flipped the page. How could such a small bag

possibly hold all of these things? She closed the notebook and handed it back to Hal.

"What's on your gay agenda for today and how can I help?"

"My what?" Hal sputtered.

"Do you really not name any of your things? Your to-do list. I'd love to help."

"Are you serious?"

"Yeah, why wouldn't I be?"

"I just got the sense that you and Alexis aren't that close. Especially with you missing her shower and bachelorette party and all the planning parties."

"Well, I'm here now. And I'm ready to work."

"Ok, great. How do you feel about flowers?"

"I don't have any feelings about them at all."

"That's perfect because I need you to do exactly what I tell you to."

Sacha gave a little salute. "Yes, ma'am."

CHAPTER 8
HAL

Sacha fell back into the snow, arms and legs spread out like an absolute angel. "Isn't it time for a break? I've been an angel all day."

Hal glanced at her watch. "It's 11:23, we've barely been working for two hours and we've only checked one item off the list."

"Right, but that one item was counting hundreds of flowers, so really it was more like a hundred items when you think about it."

Hal placed her index finger on her chin and tilted her head. "Hmm, interesting. Ok, I thought about it and have determined it was one task: checking the flowers. Sorry, but the judge's rulings are final."

"Can't we at least get a snack?"

Hal smiled and unzipped her bag. A moment later, something landed on the Sacha's stomach with a soft thud.

"I didn't know you had *snacks* in there. I didn't see those on your list." Sacha sat up and ripped open the corner of the fruit leather.

"What's that face you're making?"

"I was hoping for fruit snacks." Sacha took a bite. "But actually, this is pretty good."

"Technically, that meets all the criteria of a fruit snack."

"Do you have any other food in there?"

"Maybe. I've got to keep a few secrets. It keeps things interesting." Hal winked. There was a warm feeling spreading through her chest from the way Sacha was looking at her. Like she was the snack.

Sacha took a bite and tilted her head back. The sun caught the highlights in her hair and the line of her neck. Hal was staring, and she found she didn't care to pretend she wasn't. Sacha's cheeks were pink from the cold, and Hal had the urge to sit down next to her and pull her close. But with the way her knee was hurting, if she did that, she might not be able to get up, so instead she just observed reverently like this bank of snow was the Louvre (a stretch) and Sacha a masterpiece (true).

"What's next on the list?" Sacha's grin made it clear she'd noticed Hal's staring. Her eyes looked dark as she approached Hal, standing very close. "Something smells so good out here, like trees."

"Um, thanks."

Sacha raised an eyebrow. "I know you do a lot, Hal, but I'm not sure you're responsible for the great outdoors smelling like cedar." Sacha took a deep breath.

"Not me, but whoever made my cologne might be."

"Oh, you weren't wearing that yesterday."

"No, I wasn't."

Sacha reached up and gently brushed something imaginary off of Hal's shoulder, her hand lingering for a few seconds longer than necessary. "Well, it's very nice. So, the list."

"Right." Hal shook her head to clear her thoughts and

pulled the notebook from her bag. "Next we need to fold the name cards for each table. It's a small wedding so this should be quick and then, um—" Hal looked at the ground, avoiding Sacha's expectant gaze.

"What?"

"Then I need to go pick up the gingerbread cookies for tonight." Hal grimaced, but her eyes sparkled.

"I think there are actually a bunch in the kitchen trash, you know, if you want to save yourself a trip."

"Good point, let's throw a question mark next to that item."

"Perfect. Now let's see these cards, I'll have you know I'm excellent at folding."

"The woman of my dreams. Follow me."

Hal set the white box of cards on the dining room table. "Ok, so, one thing I forgot to mention is we also need to write out the names." Hal pulled two golden pens from her pocket with a grin. "How are you at calligraphy?"

"Why didn't you just have the names printed?"

"Because Alexis wanted the names in gold, but she didn't like the look of the embossing, which is the only way we could have the gold printed. So they embossed the design in gold, but the cards are blank."

Sacha removed the lid from the box and studied a card, turning the thick cream yardstick over in her fingers. "Um, Hal, what design?" She held the pristinely blank card up in the air.

Hal felt a tightness in her chest and yanked the box toward her. She'd checked the cards when she'd picked them up, right? Or had she only looked at the sample the printer had handed her? The printer in Detroit, hours from here. She dug through the cards, pulling out a handful and dropping them onto the table where they slid in all directions like a loose deck of cards, each one exquisitely and completely blank.

Hal dropped her head into her hands. What was she going to do? Could she drive back to the printer and get the cards? She checked her watch. No, it was already after noon. There was no way she could get there and back before the rehearsal. And it would be worse to miss the rehearsal. Probably. Though if she missed the rehearsal, she wouldn't have to face Alexis and admit this horrible, unforgivable mistake.

A hand on her knee paused her spiral. "Hal, what's going on?"

"I ruined it. Such a simple job and I failed. How did I check off 'pick up the name cards' on my list without checking them?"

"Because you're managing a lot of things. It seems like you've organized everything and not just for this wedding, but the food this week and activities. It's not a big deal, Hal, I promise. Alexis isn't going to be mad."

"But she deserves to have a perfect wedding and I've ruined it."

Sacha's hand was still warm on Hal's knee, her thumb drawing small hypnotic circles.

"Nothing is ruined. You saw how she reacted to the actual horrible cookies yesterday, right? This is nothing. Let's blame it on me. I'll think of how we can do that."

"No. I can't do that. This is on me and now I need to tell her." Hal blinked back a few tears. All she had to do was be perfect for this wedding and she couldn't do it. She wouldn't blame Alexis if she never wanted to talk to her again. She'd had one job, admittedly made up of many smaller jobs, but that's what her lists were for. Why did she spend so much time planning if she couldn't follow her own simple steps?

Sacha placed her hands on Hal's cheeks, lifting her head so their eyes met. "It's going to be ok."

Hal blinked at her. Sacha leaned forward, closing the distance between them. The kiss was quick and light, but Hal felt it everywhere, taking up all the space in her brain. Sacha Brighton had kissed her. And only fifteen years after she first imagined it. When Sacha pulled away a few seconds later, Hal leaned forward, kissing her again. She wove her fingers into Sacha's hair, holding her close. Sacha's surprised gasp when Hal ran her tongue along her lower lip made Hal's heart skip.

When they broke apart, Hal could taste the sweet mint of Sacha's lip balm on her lips. Hal opened her eyes to see Sacha looking as surprised as she felt. What had come over her, kissing Sacha like that? And what had come over Sacha to kiss her in the first place? Should she even question a dream come true?

"What was that for?"

"A distraction?" Sacha said with a shrug, but she looked away quickly.

Hal felt her stomach drop. The heat of embarrassment flamed in her face. "Right, of course. Sorry if I took it too far."

Sacha shook her head and bit her lip. "I wouldn't say that. Do you have a picture of the design somewhere?"

Hal nodded. "I think so. Yes, I'm sure I do. Why?"

"Because I'm going to draw it."

"You can't draw 80 cards and write the names, it's not possible."

"I can and I will. Did she really invite 80 people to this thing?"

"No. She invited almost 200, but only 80 are coming. Maybe less actually, since her friends dropped out. I need to update the count, but I stopped because it was upsetting her."

"Oh." Sacha's eyes were wet when she looked back at Hal. "I didn't realize so many people bailed. Okay, 80 is doable."

"The design is Todd's last name, and, well, Alexis's last name by the time of the reception. Fugg. It's in a kind of loopy script with some holly."

"No."

"No?" Hal raised an eyebrow. "I'm pretty sure that's the design."

"No, as in no, I'm not writing that. And no, as in there's no way she's taking that name. Alexis Fugg? You've got to be kidding me."

"I think the name thing was important to Todd."

"I can't believe he wants her to be Lexus Fugg. I'm just going to pretend this design is for a client I disagree with."

"Good plan. I'll go grab my computer." Hal pushed herself up from the table, only wincing a little. That morning in the shower, the bruise on her knee had been a swirl of deep purple and blue like a new galaxy.

"Hey Hal," Sacha called out as she reached the door.

She turned back. "Yeah."

"You're a really good kisser. Anytime you want a distraction, I'm your girl."

Knee pain be damned, Hal had to stop herself from skipping up the stairs to her room.

CHAPTER 9
SACHA

Sacha's hand was cramping by the time she finished the name cards, each Fugg taking away a bit more of her soul. Hal had gone to pick up the gingerbread cookies, and the cabin felt strange without her, silent and too empty. Hal was quiet and unobtrusive, but she had a presence. She was the human equivalent of a favorite candle, throwing off a warm light and soothing everything around her.

Hal's footsteps echoed in the hall. When had she memorized that sound? Sacha stood and went to meet Hal, taking the bakery boxes from her and setting them on the counter.

Hal leaned her elbows on the table and studied the name cards laid out. She still wasn't putting much weight on her knee and she had it bent adorably.

Sacha walked up behind her and put her hand on Hal's lower back, leaning against her to look at the cards too. "Would you rather sit?" Sacha moved to pull out a chair.

Hal shook her head. "No, I'm good. Sitting in the car just now made my knee a little stiff."

Sacha settled back against her, feeling the softness of

Hal's sweater beneath her fingertips. "Got it. Did you want to check these against your list and make sure I got them all?"

Hal scanned the table and picked up her list before turning to Sacha with a grin. "And what, might I ask, are all these gold check marks?"

"I *am* capable of tracking my work, you know, but it will only offend me a little if you want to double-check."

Hal folded the paper and placed it into her bag. "Very gracious of you." Hal bowed toward Sacha with a glint in her eye. "But I trust you."

"I think you might be the only one."

Hal raised an eyebrow, but the backdoor flew open, startling them both and saving Sacha from Hal's question by a far worse fate.

Sacha straightened and took a step back.

"Hello, Sacha... and Sacha's friend." Her mother was in a cream shirt suit with gold buttons and a pillbox hat. Quite the choice for her daughter's wedding rehearsal.

"Hi, Mrs. Brighton. I'm Hal. We've met a few times. At the shower, and the cake tasting, and looking at venues. And the engagement party. And a few days ago."

"Right. The wedding planner. Hello again."

Sacha's father glanced up from his phone. "Hey, champ."

"Is everything on track for tonight?" Sacha felt her mother's eyes trail up and down her, taking in her jeans and sweater before she turned her attention to Hal.

"It is."

"Great, then why isn't my daughter ready? We have to leave in two hours."

"*I'm* not ready because all I have to do is put on my dress, which will take two minutes."

"Something must be done about your hair, Sacha."

Sacha glanced at her dad, who was furiously typing something on his phone.

"What's wrong with my hair?"

Her mother blinked at her like she'd asked the world's dumbest question. "I understand that cut is your preference even though it's too short. At the very least it needs a blowout, but we'll leave that to the professionals. If I'd have known the state of things yesterday, I would have scheduled you an appointment for a cut and color, something to clean it up."

Sacha ran her fingers through her very not cheap haircut. Her hair fell at her shoulders. It was the longest it had been in years.

"Thankfully, there are hairdressers for the rehearsal." Her mother scanned her face. "And a girl to do makeup."

"Why all this for the rehearsal? Will there even be photos?"

Her mother smoothed down her skirt even though it looked fresh out of a garment bag. "With the amount this thing is costing us, there'd better be. Who gets married in a barn like an animal when the country club is so close? I feel like they should pay *us*."

Hal stiffened next to Sacha. She must have been drifting closer to Hal as she spoke to her mother, because she could feel Hal close behind her like she was propping Sacha up.

"I wasn't aware that animals got married," Sacha said.

Hal cut in before Sacha's mother could respond. "The barn doesn't have animals. It's very beautiful and most importantly, it's what Alexis wanted."

"Yes, it's Alexis's day and the rest of us must bend to her will."

Hal opened her mouth, but Sacha rushed to speak over her. Better she draws her mother's ire than Hal. "What's with the hat?"

Her mother reached up to her head and adjusted one of the gemstone bobby pins securing the hat in place. "A proper wedding deserves an elegant hat."

It had a little lace veil Sacha hadn't noticed before. The audacity was stunning. If this was her outfit for tonight, Sacha could only guess how off the rails she'd go tomorrow for the actual wedding.

"I think you're confusing this with the Royal Wedding."

Hal leaned against her and she let herself sink back. It felt so different talking to her mother with Hal by her side. The usual surge of adrenaline that always accompanied encounters with her mother was nowhere to be found. Hal placed a hand on her shoulder, bringing her mouth close to Sacha's ear. "Please go get ready. I'll handle this."

Reluctantly, Sacha took a few steps toward the stairs. "Ok, I'm off to make myself presentable for the five people we'll see tonight. Nice to see you, dad."

Her dad grunted but didn't look up from his phone. Work emails probably, like always. What did she know? Either way, paying attention to anything besides the people around him.

THE ROOM next to Alexis's bedroom had been transformed into a hair and makeup studio, that is unless this large vanity and lighted mirror had always been there? Alexis turned slowly in her chair.

"I heard you ran into mom."

"I did." Sacha gave a tight smile.

"Glad to see you're still standing. Here, put this on."

Alexis tossed Sacha a black cape. And once she'd snapped it into place, Alexis passed her an open bottle of champagne.

Sacha glanced around the room. "Where are the glasses?"

"I forgot them in the kitchen and I couldn't go back down and face mom again. I already got an earful about drinking before one of the most important events of my life."

"She knows it's just the rehearsal, right? Did you see she's wearing a veil?"

"Don't even get me started. She did mention that you and Hal were looking pretty cozy."

"She doesn't know what she's talking about. She didn't even know who Hal was."

"Oh, she knows who Hal is. She was probably just pretending she didn't as some sort of power play. She blames Hal for me not having the country club wedding of her dreams."

"Of course she does."

"Are you saying you weren't getting cozy with Hal?"

Sacha took a swig of the champagne and wiped her mouth with the back of her hand. Alexis handed her a tissue with a smirk.

"Would you have a problem with that?"

"I just don't want Hal to get hurt, Sach. No offense, but you've always been able to look out for yourself."

"That's because I had to look out for myself, Alexis. Mom and dad didn't pave the way for me like they did for you."

"They did. But you bought a Subaru and chose to go off-roading instead."

"Was that a lesbian joke? Are you saying I went into the gay wilderness?"

Alexis grinned. "I can make jokes. Look, Sach, I adore you, but you're kind of a mess. A lovable mess, but still."

"Just because I'm messy doesn't mean I'm bad at relationships."

Alexis raised an eyebrow and reached her hand out to take the champagne back. Sacha's fingers were icy where she'd been gripping it.

"Fine, just because I've been bad at past relationships doesn't mean I'll be bad at this."

"Ok, so you're thinking about a relationship with Hal?" Alexis's voice rose hopefully.

Sacha sputtered. "What? No. Maybe. I don't know. Can't we just have a little fun?"

"No." Alexis took a long pull from the champagne bottle.

"No?"

"Hal's not a fling type of person, Sach. I've spent most of the last few months with her. She's the kind of person you change your life for. Like, you start picking towels up off the floor and charging your phone so you don't miss her calls. She's worth your best."

Sacha's throat felt dry as she took the bottle back from Alexis. "I didn't realize you two were so close. Don't you have a dress to button yourself into or something?"

"These past few months Hal's been there for me more than anyone. When my friends bailed on the wedding or blew off helping, Hal was always there and she never made me feel like I was too much. I know she's working, but she's a good person, you know? She never made me feel like an obligation she was only paying attention to for the money."

"I didn't realize that about your friends. But what about Mom? I assumed she'd been micromanaging your every wedding decision from the hotel or wherever. I figured you'd be sick of help by now."

"She hasn't been involved, really."

"Oh." Sacha searched for something comforting to say back to her sister, but instead she was consumed with rage at her parents for letting Alexis down. Though hadn't she essentially done the same?

Alexis paused and blinked a few times. "Yeah, she hasn't seemed very interested since I wanted to keep it smaller. Hal's been a godsend. I'm not sure how I would have made all those decisions without her. No one ever tells you how paralyzing it can be to choose between two shades of white. Every day I'm expected to have strong opinions on things I've never cared about."

"I'm sorry, Alexis, I should have been around more, and I wasn't. I didn't think you needed me. You've always been surrounded by so many friends, and I always just felt like an extra in The Alexis Show."

"I've always needed you, Sach. You're my rock. Those friends aren't here and the second I didn't do exactly what mom wanted, she got busy with her committees. This process was a lot lonelier than I expected. I don't think I could have gotten through it without Hal. I'm so glad you're here now, truly. But please don't start anything with Hal unless you're really serious about her. I don't want to lose her friendship because you decide on a whim to move back to Chicago and break her heart."

"Ok, I understand. I won't hurt Hal."

"And you'll wait until you're sure?"

A sharp rap on the door was followed by an ice pick of a voice singsonging "I hope everyone's decent because it's time to get gorgeous."

Sacha widened her eyes at Alexis. "Alexis, what have you done?"

Sacha never realized hairspray could be heavy, but between that and a bandolier's worth of bobby pins her neck was supporting an extra ten pounds. She laid on her bed staring at the ceiling, listening to a playlist on Spotify as loud as her headphones could go. Her stomach was swirling with angst she hadn't felt since high school. She liked Hal, but she was never one to thrive under pressure.

The bed sank beside her, and Sacha looked up to see Grams smiling down at her. She lifted her headphones from her ears. The tinny sound of guitars escaping into the space between them until she paused the music.

"You might be all grown up now, but some things never change. I knew after seeing your mother you'd be in your bedroom sulking and blasting your rock music."

"It's pop-punk, but fair enough. It's not just mom. I just had a strange talk with Alexis and I'm just feeling kind of useless. Like maybe the person I am just isn't great."

"You're one of the best people I know, always have been."

"But I'm a mess. I change jobs every 9 months. I've lived in six different cities. My longest relationship ended miserably."

"Is this about Hal?"

"No, this is about me."

Grams stared at her silently, folding her hands on her lap and waiting.

"Fine, I guess it's a little bit about Hal."

"I think you'd make a wonderful couple. It's nice to see you so attuned to someone."

"But Hal is so good and I'm... me. I'm constantly messing things up and letting people down."

"Well, my love, I think you make it a point to not be very good at things you don't enjoy."

"Doesn't everyone? Why would anyone make it a point to be good at things they don't enjoy?"

"Oh, my dear. Because that's life. Or maybe it's not. What do I know? But I saw how she looked at you after you made those horrendous cookies. She wasn't looking at you like someone who had just messed up, she was looking at you like you hung the moon."

"I just don't think there's any way I can get myself together enough and be good for her, you know. I think I'm hard-wired to leave towels on the floor and never be able to find my keys."

Grams shrugged. "So maybe Hal holds onto your keys. You don't have to change to be loved, Sacha baby. Hal is clearly crazy about you."

"You think so?"

"I do. Now let's get you dressed before we're so late we're crashing the rehearsal. You can ride with me."

Sacha protested, but her grandma put her hand up like a crossing guard.

"Hal's already there setting up."

***

SACHA PULLED her grandma's powder blue Buick up alongside the wooden post and rail fence, and they looked out over a winter wonderland. A snowy path stretched to the barn lined on either side with pine trees lights strung between them.

"Do you think the witch is waiting to eat us at the end of that lane?"

"You've got to stop referring to your mother as the witch. She much prefers her formal title: The Wicked Witch of the Midwest."

Sacha laughed and let out a deep breath. "My apologies, I meant no disrespect. Did you know that Todd calls Alexis Lexus? And she lets him?"

"No, that can't be true. I hate it," Grams said with a laugh.

"It is. I think that technically makes this the Love Lexus Sales Event."

"If your sister hears that she will murder you."

Sacha laughed. "I'd probably deserve it."

Her grandma placed her hand on top of Sacha's on the maroon steering wheel and gave it a gentle squeeze. They should really bring back maroon car interiors.

"Are you ready for this, my dear? Do you have everything you need?"

"I'm ready. You look really beautiful, Grams. Is your dress new?"

"I always look beautiful. Stop stalling, we're already a few minutes late."

Sacha grabbed the hem of her dress, holding it aloft as her boots crunched through the snow.

The interior of the barn was softly lit. She spotted her mother and considered ducking behind Grams, but it was too late.

"Sacha," her mother hissed. "You've kept everyone waiting. Give me your coat." She glanced down and her mouth drew into a tight line. "Where are your shoes?"

"My shoes?" Sacha looked at her snow-boot clad feet. *Oops.*

"Where are your heels, Sacha?"

"Oh! I left them in the car. I'll run back and get them."

"There's no time for that. Just go find your sister, please, and touch nothing."

Sacha's boots squeaked across the floor, drawing the attention of several people she passed. Todd's family looked normal enough, his mother was busy mussing his hair. Her dark blue dress didn't have a matching veil in sight. As she joined Alexis waiting to start, Sacha spotted Hal studying her notebook. She looked stunning in a peacock blue suit and dark brown wingtip boots, like someone about to burst into a Motown bop. Sacha very much wished she was in a suit, even though the midnight blue dress she was wearing tonight was much better than the green monstrosity that awaited her tomorrow.

"Nice boots," Sacha said as she passed Hal.

Hal's eyes traveled over Sacha's body, and little sparks flashed through her. "You, too," Hal said, a slow grin lighting up her face.

Sacha made her way to the altar, followed by her dad and Alexis. As she walked, Owen's fingers buzzed near her elbow, trying to link their arms. She pulled her arms tightly to her sides. She never thought she'd be so relieved to reach an altar but as she took her place away from him, her relief was palpable.

The minister ran through the headings and then turned to her expectantly. Was she supposed to have the rings? No, that was tomorrow. Oh shit, her reading.

Sacha took a step forward and pretended to read off a piece of paper. "Love is great and these two babes are in love, *et cetera*."

Alexis widened her eyes and whispered, "please tell me you know what you're supposed to read tomorrow."

"Of *course*, I do. No need to worry about me."

They were dismissed and started the processional. Again, Owen tried repeatedly to grab her like a purse snatcher.

Sacha glared at him. "Why do you keep trying to hold onto me? Are you having trouble walking on your own?"

"I'm the best man, I'm leading you down the aisle."

"No, thank you."

Sacha glanced up in time to see Hal look away, laughing.

THE NIGHT AIR was frigid as Sacha stepped out of the warm barn. It wasn't the heat that felt oppressive, so much as it was the pressure. She spotted Hal standing near one of the trees on the path. She was kicking the tip of her boot into the hard-packed snow like it was an icepick.

"Look, mom, I'll try to come, but I'm just not sure I can make it this year. I'll have a lot to do after the wedding and it would be a long drive."

Sacha paused her approach. She didn't want to eavesdrop, but she couldn't stop herself from being drawn to Hal and wanting to know more.

"Yes, ok, I'll try. I'm at the rehearsal, I've got to go... Yes, I will call you tomorrow. Ok, me too. Bye."

Hal looked up and caught Sacha's eye. "Aren't you cold?"

Sacha hadn't grabbed her jacket, but she couldn't bear the thought of going back in to get it. "Yeah, but I'm just going to the car to get my heels. And a little air that's not stifling."

"Is the barn too warm? I can talk to maintenance."

"No, everything is perfect. You did a great job."

"Here," Hal said, shrugging off her jacket and wrapping it around Sacha's shoulders. "I'll go with you."

Sacha looped her arm through Hal's as they walked down the snowy path toward the cars. "How long do you think we have to stay? We've been here for hours."

"I've been here for hours. You've been here about 45 minutes." Hal smirked. "And besides, I think your sister might expect you to stay for the dinner part of the rehearsal dinner."

"You're probably right." Sacha sighed and rolled her eyes at herself. "I know I'm being a baby."

"It's been a long day. And things with your parents are hard, but it seems like you and Alexis are getting closer. Maybe you could view this family time as a favor to her?"

"I suppose I *do* owe Alexis a lot of favors. And I really want to support her. I didn't realize how much she's been struggling with our parents, too. I'm proud of her for standing up to them."

"Yeah, she's been working hard. You both have." Hal smiled at Sacha.

"Did you know earlier during the rehearsal I caught my dad playing candy crush? I always assumed he was doing work stuff on his phone, but maybe he's been playing video games this entire time."

"It's a hard job," Hal said gravely, "but somebody's gotta do it."

CHAPTER 10
HAL

The clock struck eleven and Hal was ready to turn into a pumpkin. Being in her 30s was a real trip. Now a successful night meant she was asleep well before dawn instead of after it. If she saw a sunrise these days, it was because she had too much on her mind to sleep past 5 am.

The guests had filed out, and she spent a few minutes surveying the mess and planning her attack before she started gathering the empty wine bottles to recycle. It had been another epically long day, but time felt faster with Sacha around, lighter somehow. Hal thought back to how she'd drawn out the counting and checking of the flowers because Sacha kept stopping to smell them. She'd always thought that was some elaborate metaphor, but Sacha took time to smell each one.

"Hey."

Hal startled at the voice calling out from the open door, a slow smile she didn't want to fight pulling at her lips. It was like thinking about Sacha had conjured her.

"Hey, did you forget something?"

"I thought maybe you could use some help. You've got a

big day tomorrow, too. I hope that's ok. I know you prefer to do things a certain way and I... don't."

"It's more than ok. I'd love your company."

"Good, because I already sent Grams back to the cabin, and I'd hate to walk back in this dress."

Hal scanned Sacha, her eyes roaming slowly over her hips, outlined exquisitely in the midnight blue silk of her dress, before catching herself. Manners, Hal.

Sacha laughed. "I'll take that look you're giving me as a yes. So, what's on the list?"

"Wine bottles to recycling, first. Then gathering any trash."

"Sounds like a plan. I can't believe this place doesn't have a cleaning crew." Sacha picked up a few wine bottles and placed them in the bag to be recycled.

"It does. They'll be here in the morning. I'd just rather get a few things done before leaving."

"Oh. That's, um, nice of you. You're one of a kind, Hal."

Hal frowned. "I know it can be a bit much. I just want things to be perfect tomorrow. It feels like a big presentation that I've been working on for months. I don't want to leave anything to chance and that includes cleaning up."

"That makes sense." Sacha put her hand on Hal's shoulder. "It's sweet to me how much you care about Alexis's wedding. She told me earlier what a rock you've been for her. I'm sorry I wasn't around more but I'm glad she had you."

Hal shrugged and reached for another empty bottle. "It's nothing, really. Just doing my job."

"No, it's more than that." Sacha grabbed Hal's wrist. "I'm sorry if I made things awkward earlier."

"When?"

Sacha threw back her head and laughed, wiping a tear

from her eye. "That's a fair question. In this case, I was referencing when I kissed you."

"Oh, right, that. You didn't."

"I definitely recall a kiss." Sacha stepped toward Hal and quirked an eyebrow. "Was it really that forgettable?"

"That kiss was the opposite of forgettable. And the opposite of awkward."

"So, in your professional opinion, would there be any harm in another? Just a couple of old friends."

"We were never friends." Hal's breath caught. All she wanted was to stretch this moment out, to live in it.

Sacha tilted her head. "No, we weren't." Her hand dropped to Hal's hip and pulled her closer. Hal felt the heat of Sacha through her thin dress shirt, the press of her fingers just below Hal's belt. "But we're fixing that."

Sacha leaned in a bit more, then paused, their lips inches apart. Hal could smell the slight vanilla of her lip gloss. The waiting was like a plane gathering speed on the runway, preparing for that moment it would take off into the sky. Hal let her eyes fall closed as she waited for that moment of weightless liftoff, but it didn't come.

Hal blinked her eyes open and caught Sacha's gaze. Was Sacha second guessing kissing her? Maybe she wasn't that interested. Hal took a deep breath and steadied her voice. She could ask the hard question. "Why did you stop?"

"I'm waiting for the green light, babe. I don't like to run yellows."

"Speeding through yellow lights seems like your style of driving exactly."

"Right, I'm just using yellow lights metaphorically. In the real world they mean hurry up."

Hal chuckled and closed the distance between them,

her stomach doing backflips. Sacha deepened the kiss immediately, backing Hal up until a table hit her thighs. She slid up onto the table as they broke their kiss. Sacha laid her hands on Hal's knees and she winced. Sacha's hands shot back at once and she clasped them behind her back.

"Oh, your knee. I'm so sorry. Is it still hurting much?"

"Not much, it's just bruised now, so it only really hurts if I walk into something."

"Or if someone tries to put their hands on your knees in a sexy way."

"Right, but no one's been doing that." Hal parted her knees and pulled Sacha forward. "Are you sure you're okay with this?"

Sacha nodded. "Are you?"

Hal kissed Sacha again, sliding her hands up the sides of her dress and toying with its zipper. "Definitely more than ok," Hal said, smiling as their lips met again.

***

"Are you sure it's okay we didn't get more cleaning done?" Sacha whispered over her shoulder as Hal followed her up the stairs of the cabin. Sacha's grip was tight on her hand, like she was trying not to lose Hal in a crowd. Hal felt the warm glow of protection in her chest. It was mixing with the desire that their make out session after the rehearsal dinner had stoked. She could do this. She could go to bed with Sacha. Even if it wasn't forever, it would be worth it, right? And Sacha had given no indication that it was only one night. She'd told Alexis she was living in Detroit, so there was no reason everything had to end after Christmas, like some broken spell.

Sacha paused outside her bedroom door and caught Hal

as she crashed into her. Sacha wrapped her arms around Hal's waist and placed a light kiss on her neck. "You're very quiet. Are you having second thoughts?"

"I'm good. Just trying not to wake your grandma."

"I wouldn't worry about that. Grams had a full glass of wine. Plus, I'm pretty sure she knows about sex. She had three kids."

Hal felt the heat blooming on her face, though it was more excitement than embarrassment.

"Hey, look at me." Sacha lifted Hal's chin with her finger until their eyes met. "Was that too forward? We don't have to do anything. You can just stay the night. Or not. Whatever you want."

"How about I show you what I want?" Hal leaned past Sacha and opened the door to her room before walking them backward into the darkened space.

Sacha turned on the lamp on her bedside table and Hal followed behind her. She trailed her fingers up Sacha's sides again, carefully undoing the hook and lowering the zipper of her dress. Sacha let her dress fall and kicked it to the side, turning to face Hal.

The soft glow of the lamp bathed her skin in warm light. Hal's brain short circuited as she stood staring at Sacha in her midnight blue silk bra and underwear with matching cream lace. Sacha put a hand on her hip.

"I don't want you to get the wrong idea. This," she said gesturing up and down her body, "was a very inappropriate gift from Alexis. It seems her concern about my ability to dress myself does not stop at the dress. But if you play your cards right, the set for tomorrow is even better."

"I have never been more grateful to Alexis." Hal bent down and lifted Sacha's dress, draping it carefully over the chair back.

"What are you doing?"

"I don't want it to get wrinkled."

"Hal, focus." Sacha crossed her arms over her chest, but her smirk gave her away.

"I am very focused." Hal removed her suit jacket, laying it over Sacha's dress, followed by her dress shirt and pants, which she folded to maintain the crease. Sacha might throw her nice clothes on the floor, but the thought made Hal shudder.

Finally, she stood facing Sacha in just her boy shorts and her bra. Everything about it felt illicit and Hal felt a sharp spike of panic like she was about to be caught kissing a girl in the locker room. But beneath that fear was something sweeter, something that soared through her like the hope of a great adventure. She looked up to see Sacha studying her.

"I haven't seen your knee since you fell. Your bruise matches my lingerie now. Does it hurt?"

"Not much." Hal looked down at the dark bloom of a bruise on her knee, hoping it wouldn't give her too much trouble. Though it wouldn't be the first time she played through an injury for a shot at glory.

Sacha held out her hands and pulled Hal toward her, tumbling them both onto the bed.

Hal's heart rate picked up as she leaned over and kissed her, Sacha running her tongue along Hal's lower lip. Hal didn't need another cue to deepen the kiss. She was usually intent on setting the pace, but Hal found she liked to follow Sacha's lead. Sacha wrapped a leg over Hal's hips, pulling her down until their bodies pressed together. The warmth of Sacha's body felt like pure and perfect comfort.

Their hips moved together as they kissed, Sacha's hands roaming over Hal's stomach and under her tight bra until she sighed in frustration. Hal broke their kiss and lifted herself off. "Is something wrong? Did I hurt you?"

"No, I just need all of this off, now. If that's okay with you." Sacha reached up and ran her fingers under Hal's bra. Hal nodded and Sacha pulled it off, dropping it on the floor. "Sorry, do you hate clothes on the floor?"

"Not when it's like this." Hal reached forward and unhooked Sacha's bra, setting it near the edge of the bed. She placed soft kisses down Sacha's collarbone and stomach before kissing along the lace of her underwear.

Sacha reached down and hooked her thumb into the waistband, pulling them down a bit before Hal took over and slid them off her legs. She was wavering between wanting to stare reverently at Sacha or consume her. Hal kissed her hip and then a slow path back up to Sacha's breasts. Even though she knew what she was doing, the nerves running through her like a current felt a bit like her first time, eager and uncertain and absolutely desperate to discover everything.

Hal ran her tongue over Sacha's nipple as she took her other breast in her hand. Sacha arched into her mouth. Hal made a mental note of the noises Sacha made. She slipped her leg back between Sacha's and Sacha pushed up to meet her immediately, her hands gripping Hal's shoulders.

Sacha moved against Hal, sliding her hands down to grab Hal's hips, but Hal kept her pressure gentle and her touches light.

Sacha threw her head back on the bed. "Hal, stop teasing."

"I'm not teasing. I'm savoring."

Sacha grabbed Hal's hand and moved it lower, so it was on her hip. "Please."

Hal kissed her as she dipped her fingers into Sacha's

wetness. The moan that escaped Sacha made Hal wish she hadn't waited so long. That sound from this woman was something she could listen to forever. She ran her fingers in light circles over Sacha's clit, focusing on each time Sacha arched, pressed into her, or her breath caught.

Hal looked up at Sacha, her hair spilling out of its updo and onto the white quilt. She moved her hand down, gathering the wetness at Sacha's entrance. She wanted to taste her, but there was also something so perfect about the idea of making Sacha come with only her hand. Sacha pressed up into Hal's hand and she entered her slowly.

"More, please, Hal," Sacha gasped, throwing her head back.

It didn't take much before Sacha came hard around Hal's fingers, clutching at Hal's back in a way she knew would sting a bit in the shower only a few hours from now. She cried out Hal's name and Hal brought a free hand up to cover her mouth, which Sacha promptly bit. No one had ever bit her like that, in a way that made her miss it as soon as the pain began to fade.

Hal waited for Sacha's breathing to steady and the aftershocks of her orgasm to ebb before she began to pull out, but Sacha grabbed her wrist, holding her there. "Wait, stay for a minute." Hal felt Sacha tightening around her before Sacha's body settled and Hal placed kisses over her collarbone; still salty on her lips.

After a minute, Sacha let out a shaky breath. "Ok, I'm good. Come here."

"Yes, ma'am."

Hal felt the rumble of Sacha's laugh in her own chest as she licked a line up her neck and withdrew her fingers. At the last second, Hal paused, and met Sacha's gaze before entering her again. This time Hal's movements were slow and deliberate, but not soft. Hal curled her middle finger each time she pulled back and Sacha moaned into her shoulder. Hal grabbed Sacha's leg behind her knee and brought it to rest above her hip as she continued to press into Sacha until the only sounds she uttered was Hal's name.

"Holy fuck, I can't, you can't—I'm going to be so loud."

"I think I can help with that." Hal brought her palm to Sacha's mouth and felt the sharp sting of her teeth right before she came again. Hal knew it was going to hurt, but she looked forward to it all the same.

CHAPTER 11
SACHA

The sun was streaming brightly through the curtains that Sacha forgot to close the night before. She threw an arm over her eyes and snuggled closer to Hal.

A bang on the door startled her and before she knew what was happening Hal had surrounded her, wrapping her in a tight embrace as though shielding Sacha from an explosion.

"Hal, it's ok. It was just a knock on the door. Shit, what time is it?" Sacha felt around blindly for her phone and heard it clatter to the floor as her hand hit the nightstand.

"Sacha! You need to get up, it's almost 10. That only gives us four hours to get ready. If you don't answer me, I'm coming in."

Sacha jolted into a sitting position, throwing Hal off of her. "Hold on, Alexis, I'm not decent."

"What else is new? Sacha *come onnnnn*, this is the biggest day of my life. I want to drink mimosas and watch as someone paints your nails pink."

Sacha turned to Hal, lowering her voice to a whisper.

"Hal, I need you to hide. I'm sorry, but Alexis can't see you here."

Hal looked startled, and then something passed across her face like a cloud. "Why can't she see me here?"

"She just can't know. Trust me. I'll explain later. It's not personal, I just can't deal with her reaction today."

"Right. I'll just hide so she doesn't know we were together." Sacha caught the lack of inflection in Hal's voice, but she was already up, shrugging on her robe and kicking their underwear and Hal's Sleigh Bag under her bed.

"Sacha, what are you doing in there? You have 30 seconds before I bribe the beautician to add rhinestones to your nails. I'm talking entirely bedazzled, looking like nails dipped in sugar."

"You'd better be bluffing. I'm just getting dressed unless you want to see me naked." Sacha looked to Hal with a pleading gaze, and she sighed and pulled the covers over her head. Sacha threw a pillow haphazardly on the bed to distract focus from the Hal-sized lump just as Alexis threw the door open.

"I knew you weren't naked anymore. Come on, you slept so late. I think Hal is already at the venue because she's not in her room. Here you are sleeping the day away while Hal's hard at work. Let's go. I've got Grams making you coffee since I couldn't find Hal."

"You tried to find Hal to make me coffee?" Sacha glanced to the chair where Hal's suit sat draped over the back and subtly edged across the room until she was between Alexis and the suit, cutting off her view. But this left the bed unprotected. Sacha felt a light film of sweat beading on her forehead.

Alexis studied her. "Are you ok? I can't believe you slept with your makeup on and all those bobby pins. How late did you and Hal stay to clean? Thanks for doing that, by the way. She's been taking on so much since everyone bailed and I know she appreciates your help."

"Oh, yeah, I'm always happy to help. Just, you know, making up for lost time. We didn't stay too late. Did you say there's coffee?" Sacha took a step toward Alexis and threw an arm around her shoulders, turning her to face the door.

"Yeah, downstairs, but, and I mean this in the nicest way, you really need a shower before you come to the kitchen."

SACHA MADE her way to the kitchen, her hair, still wet from the shower soaking through the button-down shirt she was wearing. A shirt she wished was one of Hal's. Instead, it was a light pink button-down Alexis had left out for her so that Sacha didn't mess up her hair and makeup by 'pulling a ratty t-shirt over her head' later. She felt like an Easter egg and not in a good way. Was there ever a good way?

Thoughts of Hal were pulling a loose string in her mind, trying to unravel this morning and that look on Hal's face. It wasn't hurt or anger Sacha glimpsed as Hal pulled the covers up over herself. It was a complete absence of expression like Hal was a robot who hadn't been powered on yet.

Grams was at the counter covering a piece of toast with jam. Sacha walked up next to her and kissed her cheek, but she didn't have to bend down to do it. She glanced at her grandma's feet. She was wearing a pair of slippers identical to Alexis's, kitten heel and all.

"Not you too with these slippers, Grams," Sacha whispered.

"Oh, just you wait. Alexis got them for all of us. For wedding day prep. See, they're peep toe so we can get our nails done." Grams shuddered and took a bite of her toast, spilling crumbs off of her paper towel and onto the counter.

"Excuse me." Alexis walked up behind them and swept the crumbs off the counter and into her palm, dumping them into the sink.

Alexis was perhaps the only person in the world who could sneak in heels. Well, except Sacha's friend Rich in Chicago when he did drag shows as Mae Flowers.

"Would you mind using a plate, Grams?" Alexis asked brightly. Her voice was a little needle in Sacha's skull.

"Alexis, my dear, I would mind. Once you're over 80 you no longer need to take requests. Also, after a lifetime of washing dishes for my family, I only dirty a plate when absolutely necessary."

"Ok." Alexis turned to Sacha and clapped her hands. "Are you ready for your gift, Sach?"

"Oh um," Sacha paused so long that Grams elbowed her. "Sorry, I'm just tired. Bring on the gift."

"I'm not sure why you're tired." Grams smirked. "It sounded like you had a very good night...'s rest."

So, Hal had been right about her grandma hearing. And hearing her because Hal had been quiet when she came in Sacha's mouth, pulling a pillow over her face like a silencer.

Sacha widened her eyes at Grams and the old lady had the audacity to mouth "Good for you" and waggle her eyebrows as Alexis grabbed a box elaborately wrapped in silver paper and tied with a ribbon from the table.

"Could you not? I don't want Alexis to know yet," Sacha whispered.

"Please refer to my previous statement about taking requests once you're over 80."

"But you're wearing those slippers, so obviously you take some requests."

"Aren't the slippers gorgeous? They'll look even better after your pedicures!" Alexis shoved the box at Sacha.

Sacha tried in vain to undo the ribbon. This was a Hal knot if she'd ever seen one. She thought back to trying to untie Hal's skates a few days ago. She'd been so worried about Hal's knee and so grateful that it was just a bad bruise. If that hadn't happened, would she still be unable to get Hal off her mind? Sacha pictured Hal putting up lights in the front yard, her mix of cashmere and woodsy gentleman, and she knew she would. She must have been struggling for a ridiculous amount of time because Grams held a knife from the butcher block out to her, clearing her throat. She grabbed a knife and sliced through the silk. Sacha pulled off the paper and dropped it on the floor, stepping on it when Alexis made a move to pick it up.

"I just thought I could fold it and reuse it, Sacha, but now it's ruined."

"When have you ever reused wrapping paper, Alexis? I don't even think you wrapped this gift. I think Hal did."

"What makes you say that?"

Sacha felt her face heat but focused on prying off the tape that was holding the box shut. These slippers were set to be launched into space. "The precision."

"Fine, Hal helped."

"That's what I thought." Sacha removed the tissue paper and hooked her index finger into one of the slippers, dangling it in the air. It was petal pink and the second worst thing she would have to wear that day at Alexis's behest. The green dress flashed in her mind. Hopefully she could repurpose it after and make a mini-golf course in her apartment. It would give her empty living room some character at last.

CHAPTER 12
HAL

Hal jogged up the snowy path toward the barn, her knee protesting and her dress boots sliding with each step. She stepped inside the sliding door and pulled it closed behind her, fishing a cloth out of her Sleigh Bag to clean off her shoes. Sleigh Bag. Would she ever not call it that now? Sacha had been on her mind all morning, even though she'd been trying to pull the covers over her to focus.

The cleaning crew had done a passable job, but the tables were pushed aside haphazardly, none of them flush with the wall, and the rustic wooden benches were in a chaotic arrangement at 70 and 80-degree angles. Hal pulled out her notebook and added "align benches" to her list. She knew she should have marked their places on the floor last night. They had been perfect. She felt the flutter of anxiety in her chest. She should have set an alarm. There was no excuse for running late on the wedding day, even if Sacha had been warm and naked next to her.

She'd rushed out of the cabin without grabbing coffee, hoping to stay out of Alexis and Sacha's way. She would text Alexis in a bit to check in and see if there's anything she needed. The cosmetologists and nail artists should be arriving just about now.

Her phone buzzed in her pocket showing a text saying, "I hope all goes well today! You're doing a great job! Sorry I didn't let you get more sleep." Followed by a smiley emoji. Hal clicked the side button to shut off the screen. Her phone lit up again a second later, "It's Sacha, by the way. I took your number from Alexis's phone because I didn't have it. How is that possible?"

It's possible because you've never asked for it, Hal thought. Then again, she hadn't asked for Sacha's phone number either, and why would she? They'd hardly been more than a room apart for days. Also, she had it on a list in her notebook along with the number of every person in the wedding party.

Hal tapped out a quick "Thanks." Her thumb hovered over the smile emoji. But she wasn't smiling, and it felt like a lie. She didn't want to hide herself, and she didn't want to be the thing that someone else hid, either.

She set an alarm to check in on Alexis in 45 minutes and got to work arranging the seating. By the time she was done, she had stripped down to her t-shirt. The suit she'd wear to the wedding was in a garment bag, ready for her to change into before guests arrived. It was the most she'd ever spent on a suit, and the navy-blue wool fit her perfectly. The tailor had made sure it didn't flare out at the hips like most women's suits did and the jacket wasn't cropped and there were no darts to be found. It had cost her a month of rent but the way she felt when she put it on was worth a year, easy.

The evergreen pocket square she'd picked out matched

Sacha's dress. She'd wanted to coordinate with the wedding party but now she felt weird about it. Like she was trying too hard to be a part of something she would never be a part of. Hal was there to do a job, and while she knew Alexis appreciated her, it was also how she was paying her bills. She was working at the wedding *not* invited to it, a distinction that had gotten blurry in the past few days but now came into sharp focus like that magical moment of an eye exam. She's been looking through number one when the entire time she needed lens two.

Hal finished overseeing the flowers and the whole time had to shove thoughts of Sacha smelling them from her mind. She turned on the lights she'd strung along the snowy path from the road to the barn. She thought about throwing down some sand, but a quick cost-benefit analysis told her Alexis would much prefer slipping to sand ruining her wedding day shoes *before* pictures. She thought back to Sacha trudging in and going through the entire rehearsal in her snow boots last night. A smile spread across her face before she could tamp it down. Hal was exhausted and hungry and thinking of Sacha still made her smile. Only now, it also felt like an icicle in her heart—sharp and numbing, a heart freeze.

When she glanced at her watch, alarm bells rang through her mind when she saw that two hours had passed, and she hadn't messaged Alexis. She must have missed the reminder. Hal pulled out her phone, but the screen refused to come to life. Another check in the win column for Hal being prepared. She should have charged it last night, but she was too busy focusing on herself and Sacha. She spent twenty minutes looking for an open outlet in the barn, but the two she found were both occupied. She made a note on her future planning list to check venues for an adequate number of outlets. And then added, "or add an extension cord to the Sleigh Bag." Just like that, her mind returned to Sacha.

HAL FINISHED SLIPPING into her suit jacket just as the wedding party began arriving. The silk lining over her crisp dress shirt was just the boost of confidence she needed to get through the next few hours of seeing Sacha. It was still an hour until the ceremony, but the swirl of activity enveloped her. She showed Alexis to the room where she could finish getting ready and apologized profusely for not checking in during the day.

Sacha grabbed her arm as she tried to excuse herself and followed her out of the dressing room.

"Hey, are you ok? I was worried when I didn't hear back from you."

"I'm good, just busy. And my phone died."

"Oh, I should have thought to charge it last night! Do you want to use mine?" Sacha pulled her phone out of her bag, carefully thumbing the cracked screen to wake it up. "It has... thirteen percent." Sacha held the phone out toward Hal.

"That's ok, thanks. Look, I should get back. I want to make sure the programs are in order and go through my final pre-ceremony checklist." Hal took a step back, putting some more distance between her and Sacha. She somehow managed to look amazing in her green velvet dress. The stylist had curled a few strands of hair left out of her up-do. She smelled warm like mulled cider. It was hard to be so close to her and still hold onto what happened this morning, but Hal had to look out for herself.

"Right, of course. Is there anything I can do to help?"

"Nope. This is my job; I've got it covered. You should go be with your sister. It's her day."

"I know that." A look of hurt passed across Sacha's face and Hal had to resist the urge to sweep a strand of hair behind her ear, a simple touch to comfort them both. She thought back to this morning. If Sacha wanted more with her, she wouldn't have hidden her.

"Ok, actually, before I forget, do you happen to know what I'm supposed to read at the wedding?"

"I thought you were joking last night when you acted like you didn't know your reading."

Sacha grimaced and shrugged. "What can I say? I excel at acting ditsy as a diversion tactic."

"I see. You're reading The Book of Love by The Magnetic Fields."

"Oh shit, are you serious? I love that song. I had no idea Alexis listened to them."

"Yeah, it's her favorite song. When we drove to look at venues, she had it on repeat the whole time in my Jeep."

"That's cute. You're a good friend, Hal."

And that one word, friend, usually what Hal strived for, suddenly felt like a door closing in her face. "Just doing my job. Can you look up the lyrics on your phone or do you need me to write them down for you?"

"No need. I know the song."

"Please look them up anyway. You might forget in front of the crowd and I really need things to go perfectly from here on out."

"You got it, boss," Sacha said with a small salute before smiling and slipping back into the dressing room.

·   ·   ·

Hal's notebook was not in the Sleigh Bag. And somehow her 20th check of the bag's pockets did not make it magically appear. She tried to remember her list, but her mind was as blank as the freshly fallen snow. Hal felt her chest getting tight like she was on one of those extreme gravity rides at the county fair where the centrifugal force held her to the wall. Gravitron.

Hal walked outside and leaned against the barn. If her notebook was gone then nothing mattered, not even her suit.

"Hey there, handsome. Is it okay if I call you handsome?" Grams approached Hal and leaned next to her. "What's got you down? I hope it's not our girl."

Hal squinted at Sacha's grandma, unsure of how much she should say. "Look Gram—I mean Shirley. It's just been a long day."

"If I can call you handsome, you can call me Grams, deal?"

Hal's laugh bubbled up from deep in her chest and sounded more like relief than amusement. "Deal. I think handsome is a nice compliment."

"Do you happen to have a postage stamp in that bag of yours?"

"Oh, I think so." Hal pulled open her bag.

"Nah, it's okay. I was just testing you. I don't even read my mail, let alone place that burden on others. I just heard you're prepared for anything."

"Well, I try to be." Hal tried to keep the confusion from her voice, was there something wrong with mail? Besides, she *liked* being prepared. And she liked to be careful.

"I'm going to take a leap and assume this," Grams said, gesturing to Hal pitifully slumped against the barn, "is related to our perfect disaster child. The thing I want to say about Sacha, and I am criminally biased, is that she tries to be good and take care of the people she loves. She might not always succeed but I've never seen her do anything to deliberately hurt someone. You don't have to tell me what happened, but if she hurt you, you should tell her. Besides being pretty, she's also a little dense when it comes to relationships."

"Sacha and I don't have a relationship."

"Ok, sure, not if you don't want one."

"I don't think *she* wants one."

"I've never seen Sacha as attuned to anyone as she is to you. She cares about you. She baked cookies and she hates baking, but that was her handing you her messy, crumbling heart. She's been under pressure with this wedding and I know she's trying not to mess up today."

Hal was quiet for a long time. The cookies were a nice gesture, but she hadn't really considered the significance. They'd been terrible, and she had assumed Sacha felt guilty about Hal getting hurt. But if she missed that, maybe there were other signs Hal had missed also. Or noticed and dismissed. Even in their brief interaction earlier Sacha had tried to help her. That wasn't nothing.

Hal turned to Grams and smiled. "Thank you, I think you might have a point."

"Honey, at my age I'm all points. And before I forget, I found something of yours by the altar." Grams pulled Hal's small black notebook from the bosom of her dress. "I don't think you want to lose this. Now, what's left to do and how can I help? All you have to do to repay me is escort me to my seat for the procession. I will not be taking my son-in-law's second-best arm."

Hal laughed and flipped open her notebook, blinking back tears, whether of relief for the notebook or hope, she wasn't sure. "Sounds like I'm getting the better end of this bargain if you ask me."

THE WEDDING WENT FLAWLESSLY. Even Todd got through his vows without error. Hal had talked to Alexis every day for the better part of six months, and those ten lines were the most she'd heard Todd say at one time.

Hal's mouth fell open as Sacha recited The Book of Love from memory. She caught Hal's eye halfway through and winked. Hal felt like her body was at war. Her heart, still tender from this morning and her talk with Grams, was falling traitorously and helplessly in love while her brain was still sealed inside its panic room.

The hour-long picture session gave Hal enough time to get the dining tables all set and double-check the name cards. Sacha had really done an incredible job writing Fugg so many times. Soon enough the guests were taking their seats and glasses were being clinked for the first toast. Sacha stood up and walked to the mic. Hal's heart caught in her throat. She took out her notebook and scanned her itinerary. A toast from Sacha was not in the plan. Alexis had never mentioned it, but the way she was smiling at her sister with tears in her eyes made it seem like she wasn't surprised or alarmed. Sacha's voice shook as she cleared her throat and tested the mic. Hal felt the nerves like they were her own. Her heart was a hummingbird in her chest. *Come on, Sacha. You nailed Book of Love. A toast should be a piece of cake.* Hal held her breath as Sacha began.

The dictionary defines love as—I'm just kidding. I

wouldn't do that to everyone in this room, only to most of you. Alexis, when you asked me to give a toast at your wedding, my first thought was who's going to want to hear me talk for five minutes. Usually, mom pays me not to mono-logue. But looking around at the faces in this barn tonight, I see that I couldn't have been more right. Maybe there's a stable with a manger in the back that would be willing to take me in, given the date and all.

And then I thought maybe it will be ok. Grams is here and she's legally obligated to laugh at my jokes.

FROM SOMEWHERE BEHIND HAL, Grams called out, "I don't remember signing anything." The room filled with laughter. Sacha waited for it to die down, shifting her weight from foot to foot. She looked precariously close to tipping over on her high heels.

BUT SERIOUSLY, *I wasn't sure why you wanted me to speak because I haven't always been the best sister. I don't always show up, and when I do, I'm usually an hour late and forgot the one thing you asked me to bring. Maybe the point is that I'm here now.*

When we were getting ready this morning, side-by-side, I remembered that time you got bangs and I was so jealous. All of your friends in middle school had them too, and I was just a lowly fourth grader who wanted with my whole heart to be just like my big sister. You waited for mom and dad to leave for dinner and then we snuck into the bathroom with a pair of scissors you took from art class and you gave me bangs. They were truly horrendous, but for five beautiful minutes before I looked in the mirror and Grams started screaming, I felt like the most beautiful person in the world. I felt just like you.

I'm so happy for you, Alexis. Spending this week together has reminded me that you are still one of the kindest people I know. And I'd do well to be more like you. We all would. Thank you for loving me despite all my flaws, and maybe also because of them. And thank you for letting me be a part of this special day. I wouldn't trade it for anything.

Sacha's voice caught and she cleared her throat.

So, to honor this occasion of your marriage to Todd, who seems great by the way, I've decided to give you a second chance. Hal, do you have any scissors in that magic Sleigh Bag of yours?

The entire room turned toward Hal. She was torn between whether she should look in her bag for her sewing scissors or just pray to melt into the floor. She cleared her throat and patted her suit pockets. "I think I might have a box cutter."

The room's laughter was cut off by Sacha's mother hissing her name.

OK, folks, our mother says the ceremonial cutting of the bangs is something we have to save for later. Meet us out back next to the manger in 20 minutes. That's where the real party will be.

Alexis, Lexus, I love you. And Todd, I am optimistic about getting to know you. Here's to the happy couple!

Hal took the deepest breath she'd taken all day. She clapped along with the crowd and used all of her willpower to resist going to Sacha and lifting her in a bear hug.

CHAPTER 13
SACHA

Hal was definitely avoiding Sacha, and it was starting to feel personal. It was a busy and stressful day for her, but she couldn't shake the chill she'd felt coming from Hal when they talked before the wedding. All she'd wanted was to pull her close by those adorable suspenders and kiss her, right there in the hallway. Something designed to hold up pants had absolutely no business being so sexy.

Throughout the ceremony, she had trouble catching Hal's eye, except for when she did her Book of Love reading, which she had nailed. Now that her toast was over—and to mild success and pity laughs—she was determined to fix whatever was going on between her and Hal. She was almost certain it was because of this morning. Her panic move to hide Hal rather than just facing Alexis was weighing on her mind. And while she could think of a hundred reasons to justify her decision, none of them stood up to the look on Hal's face when she asked. Or, well, told her to hide.

As she walked outside, Sacha's heels pierced the thin layer of ice covering the snow with a glow stick crack. The winter air was ruthlessly cold and carried the faint scent of wood smoke. It was one of the few things she loved about being at the cabin, the constant smell of fireplaces and wood stoves.

She found Hal crouching next to an absolutely enormous skyscraper of a tree. She had her Sleigh Bag on the ground next to her and was fiddling with some wires.

Hal looked up at Sacha's approach. Probably because the snow was deeper around the tree and her shoes kept getting stuck. She really needed Alexis to teach her how to sneak around in heels.

Sacha held her head high as she wobbled toward Hal like a newborn colt, ready to pitch forward at any moment. Her dress was not doing her any mobility favors at all.

"You're going to ruin your shoes."

Sacha looked down at her green velvet shoes with a ruffle and a little red bow. "If I never have to wear these shoes again, it will be too soon. If this isn't a testament to how much I love my sister, I'm not sure what is."

Hal chuckled but was fishing in her bag for something.

"Is there anything I can help with?" Sacha heard the hope in her voice. It was such a strange feeling, this wanting to care for someone instead of just be cared for. She bent down next to Hal and felt her dress snag. "It seems like the whole world wants me out of this dress," Sacha said, freeing herself from the velcro branches.

"I'm just looking for some electrical tape. I'm getting everything set for the tree lighting later."

"There's a tree lighting?"

"Did you not read your program?"

Sacha reached into the top of her dress and withdrew the cream card stock with a very Hal list of the evening activities. She unfolded it and scanned the list.

"Oh hey, dancing is about to start."

"Yeah." Hal glanced at her watch.

"Maybe I'll see you in there?"

"I'll be there in a few to make sure everything's working for the band."

"Ok, find me when you get in. I bribed Owen for his phone charger and found an outlet in the dressing room if you want to charge your phone."

"Bribed him how?"

The hint of jealousy in Hal's voice sent a little flutter through Sacha. All was not lost.

"I told him I wouldn't tell Todd the story about the most wonderful time he tried to hit on me and got totally bodied by you."

"A good deal."

THE BAND WAS loud and liked to hear themselves talk but the music, all covers, was good. Sacha danced with Grams a few times and studiously avoided Owen.

The opening chords of the Book of Love streamed through the room and Sacha searched for Hal, finding her rearranging napkins on the dessert table into perfect fans.

"Hi again."

Hal gave her a small smile. "Hi. You and Grams were very cute out there on the dance floor."

"Yeah, she's a great dance partner, but she only likes the fast songs. I was wondering if you might dance with me for this one?"

Hal dropped the napkins she was holding and a few fluttered to the floor. "You want me to dance with you? In front of Alexis and your parents and everyone?"

"I do. I panicked this morning. Alexis thinks the world

of you, Hal. And she gave me this big speech about how I shouldn't pursue you unless I'm serious and I just, I made the wrong call."

"Oh, so you're not serious."

"No, Hal, I am serious. I spent 20 minutes talking to a guy I can't stand just so he would go get the phone charger from his car because all I could think about was one small way to make your day better. So, will you dance with me?" Sacha extended her hand hopefully.

Hal nodded and started to bend down.

"What are you doing?"

"Picking up the napkins."

"Leave them please before I need to bribe the band to play this song over from the beginning."

Hal paused, and a pained look crossed her face.

"Fine," Sacha said, crouching down, "let me help."

Sacha led Hal to the dance floor and placed a hand on her hip pulling her close.

Hal's warm breath tickled Sacha's ear as she whispered, "Can you please stop trying to lead? Give me just this one song."

"Fine, but only if you let me lead when they play "Something to Talk About."

Sacha stood on the toes of Hal's boots, laughing as Hal glided down the snow path to her Jeep. Her arms clung around Hal's neck and her shoes dangled from her fingertips, bouncing against the back of Hal's coat with each stride. Over Hal's shoulder, next to the barn, Sacha watched the lights of the gigantic, Rockefeller tree swim against the night sky. She felt giddy with hope and infatuation and definitely too much Champagne.

"Hey, do you think if I wake Alexis up, she'd still be willing to cut my hair?"

"I think we should leave Alexis alone for her wedding night, cowgirl."

"I'm sorry I drank so much champagne."

"That's ok, it's your sister's wedding."

"You'll still take me home with you?"

"I'm literally walking you to my Jeep right now."

"You know that's not what I mean."

Hal paused their progress. They still had half the path to go. She placed a kiss on Sacha's forehead. "I will definitely put you to bed and stay if you want."

"Just put me to bed?"

"Yeah, you've had a lot to drink and it's been an emotional day. I'm going to plug in your phone and get you some water and aspirin and get you out of that dress."

"Well, that all sounds nice, actually." Sacha yawned and rested her head on Hal's shoulder. "The tree is really pretty."

"It is."

"Merry Christmas, Hal. I'm glad I get to spend it with you."

"Merry Christmas, Sach. You can close your eyes, I've got you."

CHAPTER 14
HAL

Hal wasn't one to be dramatic but waking up next to Sacha on Christmas morning definitely felt like a gift. Sacha was sleeping the sleep of the dead next to her. The covers had slipped down, and Hal couldn't resist the temptation to touch her. Sacha's back was warm beneath her fingertips as Hal traced a tree, then connected all the freckles she saw like they were a string of lights. If she could just stay here in this perfect moment, this would be the best Christmas she could imagine.

Sacha stirred under Hal's touch and turned to bury her face against Hal's shoulder. "I can't believe you're up so early and not hungover." Her words vibrating across Hal's collarbone.

"Well, it helps that I didn't drink."

"You didn't drink at all? What about the toasts?"

"Just seltzer. I don't really drink."

"Oh, why?" Sacha raised her head and looked at Hal. "Sorry, is that rude to ask?"

Hal shrugged. "People are always curious. I just don't

like how it makes me feel. And there's a long history of addiction in my family. I guess it's my way of protecting myself."

"Well, now I'm even more horrified that you had to deal with a very drunk me last night. Did you carry me to your Jeep, or did I dream that?"

"You sort of stood on my boots while I slid my feet, like how you might dance with a kid."

Sacha rolled onto her back and pulled the pillow over her face. "That's horrifying," came her muffled reply.

Hal pulled the pillow away and leaned down to kiss Sacha. "It was cute, though nothing compares to helping you undress. I can't believe Alexis got you lingerie with garters.

"The items holding up our clothes yesterday were doing God's work. What will it take to get you to wear those suspenders again today?"

"You liked the suspenders, huh?"

"I just like everything you've got going on, Hal."

Hal unwrapped the blanket from Sacha and moved her body until she pressed against Sacha. She'd wanted to do this so badly last night, but instead she'd helped her out of the world's sexiest, all black lace lingerie with stockings and garter belts, given her a glass of water, and tucked Sacha in.

Sacha's hands strayed to Hal's hips; the blankets crumpled beside them like an opened gift. "I've been wanting you since you woke up in my bed yesterday morning."

"Mmm," Hal hummed as Sacha kissed her neck and slipped a leg between hers.

Sacha tugged at Hal's boxer briefs. "These are very cute, but I'm voting them off the bed."

Sacha's hands stilled on Hal's hips as she looked at her

expectantly. Hal nodded, hooking her thumbs into her underwear and sliding them down.

Sacha took them from her, a grin spreading across her face. "These are incredible, I can't believe you had on underwear with T-Rex wearing a Santa hat under your serious suit yesterday and I had no idea."

"Just wait until you see what I have planned for today," Hal said, rolling Sacha onto her back and taking back her boxers. She dropped them to the floor as she lifted Sacha's hands over her head. The audible catch of Sacha's breath as their nipples brushed together sent a surge of heat to low in Hal's stomach. Hal felt the lift of Sacha's hips off the mattress and rolled into it, trailing her hand down between them and between Sacha's thighs. That little gasp again. It was like hunting for presents with your name on them, Hal was elated each time she found another one. Sacha moaned as Hal's fingers drew slow circles over her clit.

Beneath Hal's grip, Sacha moved her wrists impatiently.

"Do you want me to let you go?"

Sacha nodded and leaned up to nip Hal's neck. Hal let go of Sacha's wrist and was on her back before she could even work out what was happening.

Sacha ran her tongue over Hal's nipple, first one then the other. Hal bit back a moan.

"You can be loud; everyone is already up and down-stairs or still passed out."

Sacha threaded their fingers together and Hal opened her eyes to see Sacha above her, dark hair falling across her face. She leaned forward, pressing her body to Hal's, the heat and friction of her everywhere, overwhelming Hal's senses. Against her better judgment, she let out a moan and then reached for the pillow next to her.

Sacha grabbed the pillow from Hal's hand and threw it

across the room. It hit the lamp on the nightstand with a clatter and they both froze for a second, breathing hard until the silence stretched into an all clear.

Sacha ran her fingers over Hal's lips and Hal opened her mouth to take her index finger. "I want to hear you," Sacha said seriously. Then she lowered her mouth to Hal's neck and kissed her way down.

Sacha bit Hal's hip and she lifted off the bed automatically. Sacha seized her opportunity and wrapped her arm under Hal's hips, pulling her closer. She kissed the inside of Hal's thigh and ran a finger through her wetness. As Sacha brought her mouth to Hal, tentatively running her tongue over Hal's clit, Hal's moans grew; so did Sacha's confidence until the only thing either of them could hear was Hal chanting Sacha's name.

Hal and Sacha laid entangled in the sheets and each other, tracing patterns in the beams of sun that shone across their skin.

"We should probably get up," Hal said.

"Why? Aren't you technically done working now?"

"No, I've got a few things on my list for today. Like the brunch."

"And how about me? Where do I fall on your list?" Sacha snuggled closer to Hal.

"Hmm, let me see," Hal mused, putting a finger to her chin.

Sacha bit Hal's shoulder gently. "You don't remember?"

"Oh, now I do. You're right there on top."

"Is that because it's your to-do list?" Sacha leaned over Hal and kissed her.

Hal broke their kiss reluctantly. "As much as I want to keep kissing you, I really should get moving."

"This is the wedding that never ends. I wish I could just keep you here all day. Do you want help to set up brunch?"

Hal wrapped an arm tightly around Sacha and kissed the top of her head. "Sure, that sounds nice. I'll even make your coffee."

"Coffee and an orgasm? Maybe Christmas really is okay."

"Just one?"

"Multiple coffees and multiple orgasms, please." Sacha leaned in and kissed Hal.

Across the room, a phone rang shrilly. Sacha startled and Hal's arms tightened around her. "That's my mom's ringtone. I'll just let it go to voicemail," Hal said.

"Don't you want to talk to your mom on Christmas?"

"I'll call her later. After brunch. I told her I was working today."

The ringing stopped and for five seconds they kissed in blissful silence until the ringing started again. The frustration rose in Hal's chest and she sighed louder than she intended.

"Oh, so now you can be loud?" Sacha kissed Hal's cheek.

"How is my phone not dead the one time I want it to be?"

Sacha grimaced. "I woke up in the middle of the night and plugged it in to charge when I went to get water."

"That was very sweet of you."

"This is why I never charge my phone. You don't have to answer if it doesn't ring. You should really get it. Maybe there's an emergency."

Sacha rolled out of bed and sauntered across the room. She picked up Hal's phone from the floor and tossed it to her. She winked at Hal as she shrugged on her robe. "Sorry to cut the show short. You talk to your mom. I'll go get in the shower, so you have some privacy."

CHAPTER 15
SACHA

Sacha's stomach sank when she opened the door to her room after her shower and Hal was nowhere to be found. Maybe the call was an emergency and she had to leave. Sacha threw on jeans and a wool sweater and dashed down the stairs in her ridiculous heeled slippers. She skidded to a halt in the kitchen, windmilling her arms to keep from falling on the tile.

Grams grinned up at her from the table where she was drinking coffee and doing a crossword. "What's a seven-letter word for infatuation?"

The gears of Sacha's brain creaked into motion. "I don't know, smitten?"

"Yes, you are." Grams took a sip of her coffee.

"Have you seen Hal?"

"Yeah, she's outside putting something in her Jeep."

"Is she leaving?"

"Aren't we all leaving? Or are we wedding hostages now?"

Sacha narrowed her eyes at Grams. "I'll be right back. Use the time to make up more clues to tease me."

"You know I will."

Hal was sitting in her driver's seat with her phone to her ear. Sacha waved her arms frantically like she was trying to stop an oncoming truck.

Hal ended her call quickly, lowered her phone, and opened the door to her Jeep. "Is everything ok?"

"Yeah."

"Oh." Now that the panic of Hal leaving was ebbing, the cold hit Sacha like a wave, her wet hair felt like icicles. "Was there an emergency with your mom?"

"Not unless you count her wanting me to come home today as an emergency."

"Oh." She had to find a new word. She tried to push the pout from her voice as she squared her shoulders. She and Hal had slept together twice, and sure Sacha was smitten with her, but Hal didn't owe anyone, including Sacha, her Christmas.

"What's that look?"

"What look?"

"That look like Santa didn't come this year."

"I'm just being selfish. What else is new, right? What time are you leaving this morning? I know it's silly, but I'm going to miss spending Christmas with you." Sacha shifted her weight, wishing she'd stopped to put on boots. Or a coat. Or something in any way practical for the 30-degree weather she found herself standing in. At least the driveway was clear, and the fur lining of the slippers was doing a decent job keeping her feet warm.

"Well, good news," Hal said with a grin, "you don't have to."

"What do you mean?"

"I'll be here."

"No way. I can't believe Alexis is making you work on

Christmas Day. After her wedding is over. Besides brunch, is there anything you need to do?"

"Just a few odds and ends, but brunch is a big job. It has its own list."

"Leave the list with me—I can take care of it. You should get to be with your family."

"It's ok, really I'd, um, prefer to be here. Working... or not."

"Wait. Is the person who lectured me about the importance of family time saying she doesn't like to go home for Christmas? Is this actually something we have in common?"

"Fine. Yes. I'm avoiding it. But my family's not good like yours."

"I know my family is good, or Alexis and Grams are, but I never feel totally like myself here. I never feel at ease."

"I get that. My mom still calls me Hallie and buys me heels. It's very confusing. I guess I got to this point once we lost my dad that I didn't feel like I had much to go home for. It's hard to grimace through gifts, and it's strange how getting a gift can solidify how little someone knows you. A gift can affirm or crush you, and sometimes the only difference is the color of the shirt. Have you ever felt devastated by the color of a sweater? The gifts my mom gives me paint a portrait of all the ways I'm not who she wants me to be."

"You're right. I might not like the gifts Alexis, or my parents get me, but they don't make me feel inadequate. I just think they're ugly."

"To be fair, those slippers are pretty gruesome."

Sacha laughed. "Didn't you wrap them?"

Hal nodded and grimaced.

"So, and this might be really out there, and you can totally say no, but what if I come to Christmas with you?"

"You don't have to do that. We can just stay here."

"I know I don't have to. I want to. Alexis and Todd are leaving for their honeymoon and everyone else is driving back home this afternoon. If we leave after brunch, we won't miss anything." It wasn't Sacha's style to beg but she was feeling a strong temptation to. What would Hal's family be like? Maybe she could see Hal's childhood bedroom, filled with trophies and old notebooks filled with pages and pages of lists. "You're always doing stuff for everyone else, let me support you."

"You know I'm being paid, right?"

"Oh, am I not going to be compensated?" Sacha stepped toward Hal, stretching up a bit to kiss her.

Hal had her back pushed against the side of her Jeep in seconds.

Sacha gasped when Hal slid a hand under her sweater; the cold air nipped at her skin.

"You'd really come home with me?" Hal whispered.

Sacha nodded and pressed her body to Hal's. "I don't have any evidence of this, but I assume parents love me." The heat from Hal's body was delicious. Hal was a fire Sacha wanted to stay by all winter. Slowly feeding it to keep it burning. She ran a hand over Hal's stomach, the waffle knit like braille beneath her fingers. Sacha had never imagined wanting to tear a thermal shirt off someone before, but in this moment, she wanted to tear it right down the middle like wrapping paper. "I thought we agreed you'd wear your suspenders today."

"It was a little too folksy with this shirt, but I'll put them on after my shower."

"Fine, let's get you clean."

"And you warm."

"Do you mind if we stop by my apartment before we go to your mom's? I want to throw on something a little more Christmas-y and maybe grab a print of one of my drawings to bring as a gift. Is that weird?"

"Not at all. Just plug in your address and we can swing by there first. I'm not in a rush."

Sacha tapped her address into Hal's phone and placed her hand back on Hal's knee. This felt nice. What was the worst that could happen from meeting Hal's mother so soon?

Hal studied the updated directions. "How do you like Corktown?"

"It's cool. I'm still getting to know it, but I really like it so far. And I love exploring new neighborhoods. I haven't lived in Michigan in such a long time and Detroit has changed so much in the last decade, I barely recognize most of it except the major landmarks."

"There are a few new places I'd love to show you. Third Man Records has live music and they press the shows on vinyl that night."

"I'd love that." Sacha watched Hal study the road with intense concentration. She flipped on the blinker to switch lanes, signaling her intention to the empty road.

SACHA UNLOCKED her apartment door and flipped on a light. "Watch out for the boxes. And sorry it's so cold in here, I can't really figure out the heat."

Hal maneuvered around the stacks of boxes in the living room. "I didn't realize you had just moved into this place."

Sacha tilted her head. "I didn't. I guess I'm just kind of slow to get settled."

"Oh, this box says dresser."

"Yeah, I really need to get one of those. Have a seat, I'll only be a few minutes." Sacha gestured to a leather chair in the corner, the only seat in the living room. She opened a few boxes and dug through them, dropping the sweaters that weren't quite right onto the floor. She noticed Hal gripping the armrests of the chair, so she bent to pick up the sweaters, shoving them haphazardly into the box.

"How do you find anything?"

"What would I need to find?" Sacha pulled out a dark green sweater that complimented Hal's cream fisherman's sweater. They'd agreed the suspenders could wait for another day. It was too bitterly cold for dress shirts and Hal assured her wearing a suit to her mother's would be both overly formal and a never-ending conversation.

"Do you want me to organize anything while you grab the print you were thinking of?"

"No, you just relax, I'm almost done." Out of the corner of her eye, Sacha watched Hal pull her notebook from her Sleigh Bag and begin to write. Her brow was furrowed and she bit her bottom lip in concentration. *Probably a list of how to make me less of a mess but she sure does look cute doing it*, Sacha thought, as she headed into the bedroom to change.

HAL'S MOTHER'S house was a modest one-story ranch. When they drove past their old high school on the way there, Sacha felt a wave of nostalgia mixed with dread, like some terrible jungle juice concoction sure to make her sick.

She grabbed Hal's hand as they walked up the front path. "Is this ok?" Sacha said, looking down at their intertwined fingers. "If you'd rather just introduce me as a friend, I get it. This is all so new."

"No, this is perfect."

When they reached the door, Hal raised her fist and knocked, three sharp raps on the wooden door.

"You knock at your mom's house?"

"Yeah, you'll see why in a minute."

Hal let go of her hand and Sacha gave her a confused look. Was she second-guessing bringing her? Or just bringing her as a date?

"Actually, you should probably stand behind me." Hal shifted, partially blocking Sacha's view of the door. She rose onto the toes of her boots to see past Hal.

"Am I the one hiding now?"

"You're not hiding, I'm protecting you."

"I think I can handle your mother, Hal." Sacha rubbed Hal's shoulder. "You can relax, babe. As you know, I have years of practice with difficul—"

"That's not why," Hal said quickly.

The front door flew open and two gigantic dogs came barreling outside. They looked like St. Bernards on steroids. One ran straight into Sacha, head-butting her hip before ricocheting off the porch. Hal dove off the step, landing in a snowbank and just managed to snag one of the dog's collars.

The other dog made a beeline across the street for the most decorated front lawn on the block and promptly lifted its leg on the inflatable Little Drummer Boy.

"Rufus, get back here," Hal's mother called from the open door.

"Thanks for catching Gus, Hallie. Who did you bring?"

"This is Sacha Brighton."

"Brighton? Oh! Is she the one you—"

"Mom," Hal said in a warning tone.

Sacha leaned forward, hoping to extract the rest of that

sentence out into the public record by sheer force of will. The one *what?*

"Fine. Did you see where Rufus went?"

"Yeah, he's just dug all the hay out of Mr. O'Neill's manger. Now he seems to be burying the baby Jesus in the bushes."

"Oh, not again. Berners are supposed to be so calm, gentle giants but these two are like the Bruise Brothers. Are you a hockey fan, Sacha?" Hal's mom pulled on a pair of worn boots and dashed out of the house bellowing at Rufus.

"I think Rufus just dismembered baby Jesus. And I'm pretty sure I just saw Mr. O'Neill open his blinds."

"Oh, dang it all to heck. I'll go get the beast. Don't you two go anywhere!" Mrs. Halliday bounded off the porch and down the path.

"Well, Sacha," Hal said with a crooked grin. "Welcome to the Hallidays."

EPILOGUE
HAL (ONE YEAR LATER)

Hal held the passenger's door to her old Jeep open for Sacha. She'd left the car running alongside the curb, though she'd been waiting about 15 minutes for Sacha who had confirmed, via text, that she was "absolutely ready" 35 minutes ago. Over the course of the last year, Hal had learned that "I'll be right down" meant very little to Sacha as all time was a social construct anyway.

The door to the beautiful old brick apartment building flew open, and Hal held her breath as Sacha rushed down the snowy steps with her arms full. She rushed to the edge of the steps and took Sacha's elbow before she clattered onto the icy front path.

"Hi." Hal leaned in and kissed Sacha, subtly shifting the three tote bags in Sacha's arms to her own.

"Hi," Sacha said brightly, running her finger along the underside of Hal's suspenders. "You look nice."

"Well, someone beautiful gave me these last night with a strongly worded note suggesting I wear them as my Christmas gift this year."

"I believe I said 'please.'"

"You did." Hal nodded. "Is this everything?"

"Yup, let's hope so!" Sacha took a few steps toward the street.

Hal studied the three half-full tote bags and wondered idly why not just one, larger bag for the gifts. "Where are your clothes?"

"Oh, I just figured I'll probably get some for Christmas. It seemed silly to pack extras." There was a certain logic to Sacha's thought process that Hal had come to appreciate. She thought about her own weekender bag in the backseat filled with outfit options and her portable clothes steamer. At least she'd packed enough for Sacha to steal, considering the very real possibility that the clothes she got were an assault on her senses.

Hal opened the back hatch and placed Sacha's bags inside. "You're really sure this is everything? Gifts for your entire family? Everything on the list?"

"Oh, was there a list?" Sacha tilted her head, but a teasing smile spread across her face.

"Yes, my love, I packed everything on the list."

Hal rolled her eyes. She thought about the very detailed packing list she'd made so they remembered all the gifts. She'd even drawn little checkboxes next to the items. She wished suddenly she'd gotten Sacha a sweater that said incorrigible. Hal glanced up and Sacha blew her a kiss. "You've got your toothbrush and your slippers from Alexis?"

"Yes. Would you like to check?"

"No, I trust you."

Sacha climbed into the front seat and lowered the visor to block the winter sun.

"Did you pack socks?"

Sacha turned in her seat and looked at Hal through the open back hatch. "Everyone gets socks for Christmas.

That's a given. Underwear on the other hand... do you want to ask about those too?"

"Nah, those are negotiable."

"Well, they're in there somewhere, probably buried under the gifts. Since this is a family Christmas and all."

"Did you pack the scarf you knit for Alexis?"

Sacha's eyes went wide, and Hal felt a little victorious. "This is why lists are so important."

"I misplaced it—let's pick up a gift card on the way. We're running a little late."

Hal quirked an eyebrow. "You misplaced it? It's five feet long and bright red. And suddenly you're concerned about time? What's going on?"

"It's lumpy. I don't think she'll like it." Sacha sank back into her seat.

"It's your first scarf. Of course, it's not perfect. That's not the point. Grams FaceTime coached you through it for months. I promise Alexis will love it. "

"It looks like an Elmo that got run over in the street."

"If I'm being honest, I'm a little jealous that Alexis gets it. If you aren't going to give it to her, I'll wear it today and every day until spring." Hal smiled sweetly at Sacha.

"*Fiiiine*, I'll be right back!"

And just like that, twenty minutes later they were on the road headed to Christmas.

***

"Only an hour and 45 minutes late! Hal, you really are a Christmas miracle-worker!" Grams lifted onto her tiptoes and pulled Hal into a tight hug. "Your mom got here about an hour ago and I think she's felt like a fish out of water and well she brought the—"

Hal was body-checked to the ground. Gus laid next to her panting, his tongue hanging out and a dopey smile on his face. She sat up quickly. "Two dogs tackled me, right? Where's Rufus?" Gus rolled over and pawed at Hal, giving her his belly, which she patted absently. The gust of cool air from the door answered her question. "Not again."

Rufus was going buck wild in the front yard, barrel rolling through the snow and head-butting all of Santa's reindeer.

"Should we get him?" Sacha asked.

"I think we should just let him tire himself out. Let's go say hello to everyone." Hal shut the door and bent down to unlace her boots. She slid on her slippers and reached to take Sacha's coat. Sacha kicked off her shoes and dropped her tote bags on the floor as she shrugged out of her jacket.

"Something smells good. Hi, Grams." Sacha kissed her grandma's cheek. "Merry Christmas."

"Merry Christmas, my love. Did you remember your knitting needles?"

Sacha squinted. Hal leaned over and stage whispered, "It's ok, I brought mine."

They made their way into the den. Hal's mom was sitting on the couch with Todd, laughing at a video on his phone. Hal paused at the strange sight. "Hey, Mom. What are you two watching?"

"Hi, dear." Mrs. Halliday smiled up at her.

"Hockey bloopers," Todd said, pausing the video. "Hey, Hal. Hi, Sacha."

"Hi, Todd, Merry Christmas," Hal said with a little wave. Strange that her mother had something in common with Todd, but someone was bound to, sooner or later.

"And happy anniversary!" Alexis called from the kitchen a moment later.

"Hi, Lexus. Merry Christmas and much more importantly Happy anniversary!" Sacha called back with an indulgent smile.

"Sach, come help me with these drinks. Grams made us wait for you to open presents."

"Wow, that's barbaric," she said, walking toward the kitchen.

Hal settled onto the floor near the tree and Gus plopped down next to her, taking most of the ornaments off of the lower branches. "Hey, you little gigantic baby." Hal scratched his ears.

Sacha came into view, balancing a tray of drinks like she was walking on a tightrope. She widened her eyes at Hal before slipping back into a neutral expression.

She set the tray on the coffee table and handed Hal a mug of cocoa. "I added extra marshmallows to yours. Don't tell Alexis. She was trying to ration them for *a really fun game later.*"

Alexis clapped her hands as she walked back into the room, startling Gus, who crushed several presents in response. "I thought we could all go around and say our favorite part of the wedding last year."

Sacha turned to her sister. "Alexis, are you serious?"

"Of course! It will be so much fun. You start Sach!" She perched on the armrest of the couch next to Todd.

"Fine, my favorite part was when we ate gingerbread cookies that didn't poison us."

"*Sachaaa*, think of this as your gift to me."

"Ok, great. I'll get rid of the other gift. I liked the part where you got married, too."

Alexis rolled her eyes. "Hal, what was your favorite part?"

"I loved feeling included, like I was part of the family

and not just working. But for the actual wedding, I know I'm biased, but I still think about Sacha reciting The Book of Love during the ceremony. Did you know she didn't even know what readin—"

Sacha elbowed Hal and gave her a tight smile. "Babe, please do not tell her I didn't remember what reading I was doing on the most important day of her life," she whispered.

"That's so sweet, Hal." Alexis smiled at Hal, her eyes misty. "Grams, your turn!"

"I loved how beautiful you looked."

Alexis grinned at Grams, then turned to Todd. "Ok babe, your turn."

A scratching noise like a wood chipper cut through the room and Todd leapt off the couch to get the door. "Somebody else can go," he called behind him. "Hey, Rufus," Todd said as Rufus came barreling into the room and shook his body, which was completely matted with snow.

"Hal, can you grab him and dry him off?" Mrs. Halliday asked. "There's a towel by the back door."

"I think I'll need a broom—he looks like a sherpa lining."

Sacha laughed and stood. "I'll help. We can clean him off on the porch."

BY THE TIME they came back in, Hal and Sacha were freezing and caked in most of the snow from Rufus's fur.

"Ok, you're back. That took forever. I'll pass out gifts." Alexis stood from the couch and practically skipped toward the tree.

"Where are Mom and Dad?"

"They had a thing they said they'll stop by later for

drinks if they can. But don't worry, they dropped off gifts yesterday."

"I wasn't worried. Let me help you with those."

Alexis and Sacha passed out the gifts and the world's most careful unwrapping began, except for Grams and Sacha, who shredded every scrap of paper that came into their orbits.

Alexis handled the misshapen scarf surprisingly well. Hal caught Grams beaming at Sacha. Sacha was truly terrible at knitting, but Hal thought she stuck with it only for the weekly video calls with Grams. Once the gifts were done, the others headed into the kitchen for lunch.

Hal stood up to follow them, but Sacha's fingers wrapped around her wrist, stopping her.

"I have one more thing for you, hold on." Sacha stood up and grabbed another one of her tote bags and pulled out a small box that she'd wrapped herself.

"Is it one of the 'We hope your Hal-idays are Brighton' Christmas cards you threatened to make?"

"Maybe." Sacha grinned.

Hal studied the box for a second, trying to chart a course through the truly excessive amount of tape.

"Just tear the paper." Sacha bounced on the balls of her feet.

Hal ripped off the blue paper and opened the box, furrowing her brow. "What is this, babe? I've had a key to your place since February because you're always losing yours." She pulled the key out of the small box. "Wait, it's not even cut to fit a lock—I didn't realize they even let you buy them like this."

"Sure, why not?" Sacha shrugged.

"Because it doesn't open anything like this." Hal turned the silver key over in her hand.

"Well, we don't know what lock we'll have in our new place. So, I guess it opens possibilities?"

Hal let the words settle over her, hope swelling in her chest. She leaned over and pulled Sacha into a kiss. "Not enough people realize what a sentimental nerd you are."

"Not so loud, babe. Alexis has bat ears." Sacha winked at Hal. "You promised to keep my secrets."

"And when did I do that?" Hal pulled Sacha toward her. Should they get a two-bedroom or three so they could both have offices? A place with hardwood floors and lots of windows for her plants would be nice. And a lot of closet space for Sacha's stuff.

"It's implied." Sacha wrapped her arms around Hal's neck. "What do you think? Can you really live with my chaos?"

"I can. Do you think you can deal with my lists and organization?"

Sacha tilted her head. "Hmm, knowing where to find things will definitely take some getting used to."

Hal leaned forward, and their lips met. The kiss was gentle but full of promise. "You really want to do this, live with another person?"

"No, Hal. Not another person. Only you."

The End

THANK YOU!

Thank you so much for reading Checking It Twice! As an indie author your support means everything to me! If you enjoyed this book, please consider leaving a review—they're a huge help! If you want to know about what's coming next, you can sign up for my newsletter on my website: www. lucybexley.com

CONTINUE READING FOR A
PREVIEW OF NO STRINGS, LUCY'S
NEXT NOVEL

NO STRINGS

a lesbian romance

Lucy Bexley

SYNOPSIS

Fun is the one thing **Elsie Webb** takes seriously. Though she'd be having a lot more of it if Haelstrom Media paid her enough to actually get out of debt. She's determined to hold out on contract negotiations for her kids' television show Fangley Heights until she gets what she deserves. There's only one problem, the head of the network just died and left her future more uncertain than ever.

Forty-eight hours and one funeral–that's all **Jones Haelstrom** has to get through before she can return to her life in LA that's as ordered and sparse as an IKEA showroom. When she steps in as CEO of her father's media company, Elsie Webb is her first problem to deal with. Elsie ends up challenging Jones in ways she never could have predicted, starting with an attraction neither can avoid.

As their attraction teeters on the edge of something more both agree to keep it casual. A no-strings agreement and disclosure to HR should be enough to keep things between Jones and Elsie from getting tangled, right?

CHAPTER ONE
ELSIE

Was hitting someone with a puppet technically assault? Elsie's mind said yes, but her heart—and hopefully a jury—said no. She didn't want to risk hurting the star of the show, even if he was made of felt. Not to mention, that bundle of fabric and stuffing kept a roof over her head. Elsie grimaced. She didn't really think of Fangley like that—he was a more realized person than half of her colleagues.

The set of her show Fangley Heights was gearing up for a day of filming and Elsie was already nearing her limit.

"Stop trying to control the puppet. Relax. Let *it* control you."

Elsie cringed as Trey's hand came to rest on her shoulder like a small, hot pancake, lingering for a few scorching seconds before it slid off. Trey used his hypnotist's voice, something he'd learned from one of his afternoon acting workshops. Soft and wispy and boring as hell.

Elsie had to admit it was effective. Talking to Trey did make her want to pass out to escape any further interaction with him. His personality was a constant interruption. It was like he couldn't resist talking when she was trying to focus. Her entire job was to control puppets, and he was trying to make it into some kind of metaphorical, New Age thing instead of what it was: skillful manipulation. These puppets didn't even have strings.

As the nephew of the Haelstrom's second in charge, Trey was the network's golden boy even though Elsie carried the show and frankly, she was reaching her limit with being anyone's second choice. And okay, so maybe there was that one time she had insulted some 'important' sponsors by comparing their conversation to oyster crackers that have been in an old woman's purse since the Great Depression. So dry she was left choking on their dust. But still, people didn't give second chances anymore? Was it too late to stick a stipulation in her contract for next season that Trey's puppet, Smirch, would meet an untimely end? To date, giving Trey's puppet the worst possible name was her proudest accomplishment. Even if it was technically her roommate, Avery, who had come up with it during a partic-ularly intense game of Jenga.

Elsie took a deep breath to keep from laughing at the memory of Avery knocking over the tower in exuberance when the name occurred to them. She checked her monitor as she raised her right arm over her head and above the small wall in front of her. One thing they don't tell you about puppeteering is, it makes your shoulders look great. Like seriously ripped. Well, mostly just the one shoulder, but still they should put that in the drama school brochure. Maybe she could contribute that tidbit so they'd stop asking her for money, which they absolutely knew she didn't have.

"I think if you just loosen your wrist, you could—"

Elsie sliced her gaze at Trey.

His warm whisper washed over her face and she shuddered. With her headset over her ears, she couldn't hear most of what he was saying, a small mercy, but the fact that she could see a bit of sweat on his forehead made his proximity vaguely threatening. What she'd like to do was control him. She'd donate him to Goodwill.

Elsie glanced back down at her monitor. Trey's fingers seared her skin as they wound around her wrist. His new gold watch jangled. She added 'demand a raise' to her running mental list of contract negotiation points. Elsie had a good feeling that all she had to do to get all the stipulations she wanted was to hold out for a few more days. The network would cave, she just knew it.

She took a deep breath and lowered her headset. "Are you trying to derail my entire process?"

"You just looked like you needed my help keeping this little guy steady." Trey reached up to touch Fangley. *Nobody* touched Elsie's puppet. She flicked her wrist so Fangley's hand smacked Trey's forehead before he had the chance. He blinked at her but made no move to call the authorities. So hitting someone annoying with a puppet technically wasn't assault, just as she'd suspected.

Rebecca, the showrunner, poked her head through the studio door and called Trey over. Elsie felt the tension drain out of her. Even Fangley's shoulders relaxed.

Elsie used the momentary peace to ready herself for the scene they were filming that afternoon, the one where Fangley and his cat sidekick, Ratatouille, put on way too much makeup in an attempt to fit in. The beautiful thing about the show was that its connection to reality could be tenuous as long as the bits were engaging. For example, why would a blue-tinted young vampire like Fangley and his Maine Coon sidekick think doing a full clown face of makeup would make them *less* conspicuous? Either way, she was looking forward to the arrival of Gabby, Ratatouille's handler.

The Fangley universe worked on a perfect kind of logic: very little of it.

Fangley Heights was in its third year of production. Most days Elsie couldn't believe her luck. She had picked essentially the most unemployable major, despite her father's desire for her to do something respectable. What he really meant was something with a high earning potential. Her father saw money as a down payment toward happiness, but he always forgot about the mortgage. Elsie had found no correlation between respectability and the size of her bank account. Quite the opposite, actually. Besides, she literally couldn't do math or handle bills. Even calculating tips was beyond her. On the other hand, the idea of saving people made something catch in her chest. So business and medicine were out. Her father wanted her to be employable. She wanted to be happy. But on *Fangley Heights*, most days she was both. Now if only everyone she'd ever met would stop making weird jokes about her being a puppeteer. At the very least bad jokes should be original.

But there wouldn't be a job, puppeteer or otherwise, if she couldn't get next season's agreement worked out. With each contractless day she barreled closer to an uncertain future.

She'd pushed her luck in negotiations, but why shouldn't she be better compensated? Fangley was her intellectual property, even if Haelstrom Media owned the trademark. Though it felt hard to say where everything would land with that in light of Hunter Haelstrom's recent passing. That little vamp went all the way back to a web series she'd done to kill the time she should have spent memorizing Hamlet in grad school. A little something productive to assuage her guilt over wasting time.

Her classmates tried to dismiss children's television as fluff, but this wasn't Punch and Judy hour. *Fangley Heights* had depth. It had whimsy with slightly charred edges. It only barely made sense. It was a show about an orphan vampire being fostered by a family in Brooklyn—a true American story. When Haelstrom Media had reached out to her just before graduation, she couldn't believe her luck. Elsie had felt so sure signing that contract would be her golden ticket, but she was young and naive. She didn't understand sub-clauses and percentages or that one paragraph they always threw in that stipulated media appearance requirements.

Maybe they'd learned their lesson after her season one sponsor disaster. She wished now she'd read that contract, committed every line to memory. Been asked to do a series of complicated crosswords before signing it. But she hadn't, because this was back when she still trusted people to do the right thing. She thought she'd pay off her loans, buy an apartment, and stop worrying about getting by. And yet, they were wrapping up season three and she was still sharing a place with Avery. Treating themselves meant the fancy two-for-one egg roll special.

Elsie was struggling, even though her character was a cultural icon to kids everywhere who were still learning to tie their shoelaces. Fangley was a celebrity. If a puppet could be a celeb. What was she saying? *Of course* a puppet could be famous. Oscar the Grouch? Rizzo? Iconic. Plus, as a nine-year-old vampire desperate to fit in, Fangley was relatable. For the pun-filled *Make-Over-Done* episode, Elsie had spent a solid week working with their local designer and props team on *Drag Fangley,* as she'd been thinking of him. He looked almost frightening this way, just this side of familiar, like a woman in a facemask. A ghoul you could trust.

Elsie studied Fangley and wondered if she should have let the costume department and designers just craft a mask for him. They had made some latex prototypes to mimic a cold cream and blush treatment, but they all looked too much like meringue, the cold cream mask crested in waves. And when Elsie had done a run-through of the scenes with Fangley and the mask, none of his expressions had been visible. Which upped the creep factor considerably past the tolerance of their kindergarten focus group.

The creation of a new Fangley had set them back several weeks and Rebecca warned they were approaching a meeting-with-the-boss level of being behind schedule. All of that was up-in-the-air now with the new boss still being uncertain. But Elsie had a good feeling about today. The "makeup" could be layered on individually to the new version of Fangley; she had the blush and eyelashes lined up on a table behind the wall of the set. Everything was ready to stick on Fangley's ghastly face. They'd be taking a Mr. Potato Head approach. There was probably a merchandising opportunity here, not that she was giving those ideas away to Haelstrom Media for free anymore. Elsie was still waiting to see any income from her point zero five percent share of sales from trademarked Fangley merchandise.

Elsie set about her pre-rehearsal routine. The choreography of puppets was intense. Like synchronized swimming, or one of those two-piece horse costumes. Reliably, Elsie was the ass of their outfit. In this week's episode, Amanda was playing Fangley's next-door neighbor and Trey was playing Fangley's nemesis, the elementary school's suspicious science teacher. A perfect role because it was easy for Elsie and Fangley to get into the mindset of hating him.

Elsie racked her body over the foam roller, extending her back and listening to it creak and pop as she raised her arms over her head. They had an area off to the side of the set for the explicit purpose of working out the kinks that came with contorting their bodies into puppeteering postures. Sometimes it took hours after a shoot for the stiffness in Elsie's torso to fade to tolerable. She brought her hands to the ground, bracing into a wheel shape. There was a whiff of the medieval about modern-day self-care; facial peels, cooking yourself in the sun, stretching your body over a cylinder until it gave way with a series of satisfying cracks. Torture therapy.

Elsie stood slowly, like she was being raised to standing. She punched in her code and freed Fangley from his case. The puppets sitting in a row in their glass enclosures, like little lockers, reminded Elsie of babies in a hospital nursery. Tempting to snatch but constantly monitored.

Elsie set Fangley on the fake stone wall as she considered his outfit. In an increasingly routine bout of interference, the network had insisted on Fangley wearing his black cape even though that made no sense if he was trying to fit in. Everyone knew Fangley preferred to only wear his cape at home, it was a comfort item, like a blanket. But there was concern from 'certain sectors of the market' that kids were forgetting that Fangley was a vampire because the show was doing too good a job of humanizing him. Even though vampires are human, technically. Though in this case, everyone's a puppet.

The door to the fake brownstone creaked open, and out stepped Trey. His conversation with Rebecca must have been brief for him to already be back on set; Elsie hadn't realized they'd finished talking already. So much for her break.

Now she was left to wonder how long Trey had been there, silently observing her? Add that to the list of things it was better to never know. Maybe the network should be more concerned about humanizing Trey.

He hopped down the stairs from the front door to the stage and clicked his heels. In her head, Elsie watched a fantasy of him slipping on a banana peel. Ah, the power of imagination.

"So are we going to do this scene, Els? I've got a good feeling about this afternoon."

"I always come to work, Trey."

"As long as you don't throw a fit about outfits again." He reached for Elsie's shoulder but pulled his hand back as though her arm had been replaced with a bear trap. So, he had the ability to read body language after all.

"Having an opinion isn't throwing a fit. Are you going to throw a fit about your lines?" Trey's secondary character, Myrtle, was slated to be roped in by Fangley to help fix his makeup disaster in time for the spelling bee.

"No self-respecting ten-year-old girl would go along with Fangley's makeover plan."

"As someone who was once a ten-year-old girl, I can confirm that they're usually not very self-respecting."

Elsie breathed a sigh of relief as the director walked onto the set. The official signal that filming was about to start. Only Trey could be less annoying playing an evil puppet named Smirch than as himself.

THEY WERE deep into filming the second scene, the one with Trey's character, when he tripped over Elsie's not-at-all outstretched leg and they had to pause for the day. As they broke and the crew brought Trey ice, Rebecca waved Elsie over to the production control room.

This would be a good opportunity to get Rebecca's advice on her contract woes. Though the way her forehead was doing a Shar-Pei impression gave Elsie pause. Maybe she could see if the props department still had some of that cold cream from *Drag Fangley* on hand.

"So, I've got some bad news." Rebecca gave her a tight smile.

"Okay." *Shit.* "Is everything alright with Fangley?"

"Yes, of course. He's a puppet." Rebecca looked at Elsie like she was ridiculous for caring about the vampire that was literally keeping them both in a job. Millions of people cared about Fangley. He even had his own fan club: The Fangers. Not a name she would have chosen, but the fanbase of five-year-olds were not to be swayed.

"I just got word from the network, and well, you're aware that Hunter Haelstrom passed away last week, right?"

"Yes, it's very unfortunate." Elsie nodded. It was one of those things that was sad in the *royal we* sense but not necessarily upsetting to her personally.

Rebecca shrugged. "He was in his 80s and never once looked me in the eye."

"Okay, so marginally sad. I assume some people are very upset. I didn't really know him, aside from the name on my check. Do you have any idea who's taking over? Have you heard anything?"

"I'm pretty sure the will named his widow. I've only met her once, at the Christmas party two years ago, but I got the sense she wasn't a fan of the work we do here on the Heights. Did you meet her there?"

"Oh, I think I was sick that day." Elsie shrugged. She probably had been sick—sick of absolutely everything going on at work. "Do you think she'll change the show? I mean, she wouldn't, right? The numbers are good and growing each year, but I don't trust Stu for a second not to try to oust us."

Rebecca raised her hands. "I don't have any information. I know these things aren't always logical. We should take every opportunity to make sure she knows how amazing this show is. And I think it's in our best interest to get this season wrapped this week even if it means spending a few nights together. I don't want Stu to see even the tiniest window to give this show to Trey."

"I don't mind pulling all-nighters, but you know I have a no-overnights-with-Trey policy." Elsie shuddered. "Besides, who will get Trey an air cast? He might even lose the leg."

"I've never met anyone who applies soccer foul performances to real life. Once I saw him get a paper cut and fall to the ground asking for stitches."

Elsie caught the gleam in Rebecca's eye. She almost never let loose on Trey. Rebecca was in her 50s and the consummate professional. At work, anyway. Rebecca at Chewy's, the bar down the street, was a delightful person to spend time hating things with.

Elsie wiped a tear of laughter from her eye and took a deep breath. She loved mean Rebecca. Was there anything more soul-nourishing than shit talk? "I'm so sad I missed that. Next time keep the camera running. We can add it to his showreel. Maybe get him some more dramatic roles."

"Noted." Rebecca's face sobered. "I think it's critical for everyone to sign and lock in their contracts. Please tell me you're not still dragging your feet on yours." Rebecca looked at Elsie like she was going to explain why she wasn't mad, just disappointed.

Elsie grimaced.

"I mean it about your contract, Elsie. You need to sign."

"Signing it is me saying it's okay to treat me this way. To underpay me while making a killing off of my ideas." Elsie's last contract draft had been an offer so laughably low that she'd used it to sop up her spilled Lucky Charms milk.

She had *created* the show, and yet every year it felt like she was begging them to pay her enough to buy fresh vegetables. The fact that an apple in Manhattan went for ten dollars was beside the point. Then again, wasn't some money better than no money at all? That's what Avery would tell her. *Just keep us in bubble bath and bubble tea, babe.* Maybe if the show went up a little and met her halfway she could consider maybe, possibly, signing her name on the dotted line. Which was always a solid line, actually.

"I know you wanted to hold out for more money, and I think they're ready to meet you at..." Rebecca glanced at her iPad. "Seven percent below your ask. I'd take it if I were you."

All wavering drained from Elsie. *Seven percent BELOW her ask?* Were they absolutely fucking with her? Last week it was five percent. She planted her feet. Absolutely fuck that. "That's a worse offer than before. How much below Trey's ask are you advising him to take?"

"Even if I had all the details, *which I don't*, you know I can't discuss the specifics of other people's contracts." Rebecca's eyes flitted to the monitor in the control room that showed Trey sitting on the floor holding ice on his ankle and scrolling through his phone.

"Right, because telling me how much I'm being screwed

would be grossly unfair to you and the network." Elsie turned to leave. She had an overwhelming desire for this day to end.

Rebecca caught her arm. "Look, just think about it, okay? This show matters so much to all of us. I don't want to see your dream crumble."

But Elsie *had* thought about it. Fangley Heights was her baby. The only thing she'd ever invested herself in fully. But if she could love something she created this much, who was to say she couldn't do it again? She thought about the notebook on her desk, full of half-finished sketches and jokes that brought tears to her eyes. That had always been her barometer for good ideas—what reaction they sparked in her. If she didn't find her own jokes funny, why would anyone else?

Elsie pushed open the door. "Trust me, Rebecca, this is far from my only dream." The door clattered behind her. If drama school had taught her anything, it was the power of a dramatic exit.

ACKNOWLEDGMENTS

G, thanks for all you do so I can write terrible jokes on the internet and also in word documents. It's a dream come true. Thanks to my dog, Copley, you were always there for me writing this book. Sometimes, like now, you were literally on top of me. My cats contributed all typos.

Bryce, thanks for all the commas and for putting up with my sass. Thanks for supporting my muppet MC idea and all my other questionable ideas.

S, your writing is an inspiration and your friendship is a gift. Thanks for reading this story and encouraging me. I can't wait to read what you write next and everything after that.

Luci, your friendship has been such a gift this year. I can't wait to explore Death Valley and stop at every weird tourist trap with you. Thank you for all of your help with this book!

Shauna, thank you x 1,000 for being a kind stranger on the internet. You absolutely know what you're doing. Please accept two giant dogs as a token of my gratitude.

L.I.L.Y., you support me and everyone else. I think you're a superhero. I'm honored to be your friend-wife.

To the Dad Jobs, you are the best thing that ever happened to my writing life. I cherish all of you and our group.

Anna, thanks for encouraging me to write in the first place. I can't believe you're still putting up with me.

Amanda, you're incredible. Thanks for brainstorming with me on this one and for editing this book. I love our calls and all the jokes with A.

Em, Anita, and Jess, thanks for looking at drafts of this cover. It's really different for me and your encouragement helped a lot.

To all my twitter pals, you make my days brighter and support me at my most absurd. Your friendship is a gift I don't take for granted.

If I forgot anyone it is only because I am very tired.

Most of all, thanks to everyone reading this! None of this would be possible without your support.

ABOUT THE AUTHOR

Lucy Bexley writes romcoms where queer women trip over things and fall... in love with each other. Her stories balance laughter and love with real-world struggles such as anxiety and addiction. Lucy lives in Boston with her partner, pets, and several cases of seltzer. She's the author of best-selling sapphic romances including No Strings and Must Love Silence. When she's not writing jokes in a Word doc, she's writing them on Twitter.

www.lucybexley.com

www.ingramcontent.com/pod-product-compliance
Lightning Source LLC
Chambersburg PA
CBHW020040310726
48970CB00007B/2349